FAMILY FIRST

Harrisburg Railers, 13

A Christmas Railers Novella

RJ SCOTT

V.L. LOCEY

Love Lane Books

Copyright

Family First (Harrisburg Railers #13)

Copyright © 2023 RJ Scott, Copyright © 2023 V.L. Locey

Cover design by Meredith Russell, Edited by Sue Laybourn

Published by Love Lane Books Limited

ISBN - 9781785646300

All Rights Reserved

Family First

An injury threatens to end Stan's career. Will he choose to fight for his beloved hockey, or put his family first?

Few goalies are as dedicated as Stan Lyamin, known for his resilience on the ice, talking to his pipes, and his love of Elvis. Add in his adoration of his family and his life has been filled with all the things that bring him joy. However, after a heart-wrenching game ends with a disastrous hip injury, Stan faces the most challenging obstacle of his career: surgery, an extensive recovery, and the looming threat of retirement. It's now that he has to decide which path to take: the one that will lead him back to the game he adores or the one that will see his jersey lifted to the rafters.

Erik and Stan, once invincible with the Railers, have always skated through life's challenges hand in hand. Their love story, cemented by a shared passion for hockey and the joy of raising their children, has been their shield against the world. But when their son Noah's life is changed forever by a medical diagnosis, this forever love is put to the test. Erik turns to his husband for support, but Stan is consumed with guilt, overwhelmed by decisions, and retreats into himself when his family needs him the most.

Dedication

To my family who accepts me and all my foibles and quirks. Even the plastic banana in my holster.
VL Locey

Always for my family.
RJ Scott

Christmas

A RAILERS NOVELLA

Family FIRST

RJ SCOTT &
V.L. LOCEY

Love Lane Books

Prologue

"It's always a thrill for us up here in the rafters to get a new member of the broadcast team, especially when that newbie employee is one of our Railers alumni. This man really needs no introduction to all the hometown fans watching us at home or streaming us on the Railers app, but I'm giving him one anyway. Let's give a hearty Railers welcome to Max van Hellren."

"Thanks, Dusky, it's great to be able to be a part of the broadcast team. And congrats to you too on moving up from between the benches to being our new play-by-play man."

"Aw, thanks, Max. While we were all saddened to see Chippy move on after his two-year stint here in the broadcast booth, we're wishing him all the best of

luck as he takes the reins as associate coach down in Washington. You played for a few years in D.C., Max, what do you think of this rebuild team that the Railers are going up against tonight?"

"Well, they're young and fast, perhaps too young, Dusky? They're boasting to one and all that they have the youngest roster in the league, which is wonderful in some regards but there is no contest for age and wisdom, especially when entering the first round of the playoffs as we are tonight."

"I couldn't agree more, Max. And to that point let's sneak in our goalie comparison after one period while maintenance works on a lighting issue at the Railers end of the ice."

"Yeah, I see tonight's match-up in net as something that will prove my earlier point about experience in high stakes games. Rob Ralston is only twenty-four years old, and while he has done a great job helping his team get to this first round of the playoffs, he has zero postseason knowledge, and in warm-ups I could see his nerves. They were really evident in the first period, but he did settle down after facing some sound shots from the Railers offense. Now, on the other end of the ice, we have the veteran Stan Lyamin. Stan has been down this road more than

a few times. Heck, he's been there and bought the T-shirt."

"Right you are, Heller, if you don't mind me using your nickname?"

"Nope, call me what you want just don't call me late for dinner. That's a jokey thing my husband Ben and I have. I like to eat."

"Ha! Well, you look well-fed and happy, Heller. It's going to be an exciting game if we see Stan come into the series in good health. So far he's looked good, and the word from the Railers goaltending coach, Pat Yannerman, who joined the team just this past fall, is that Stan is at one hundred percent. While he didn't really have to do too much in that first period, he did look solid on his skates. But the past few years have taken their toll on the thirty-nine-year-old goalie. He's suffered through some groin issues, as well as several undisclosed injuries that many are whispering might be hip problems. If Lyamin is feeling up to par I do not foresee this young Washington defense being able to shake him at all. But if he's feeling his age, and you and I both know how that feels, Heller, he might be an easier mark for the sharpshooters Washington has brought to Harrisburg."

"Ha, yeah, I can attest to that. I have the heart of

a teenager and the body of an octogenarian. Ah good, we now have all the lights on so the second period can commence. Looks like the Railers are sending Tennant Rowe in to take the face-off, Dusky. A good move. Rowe has led the team in face-off wins all season, and tonight he's already gone ten to one against the usually highly competent Pierre LaVou."

"It's always a joy to watch Rowe play. Second period underway. Washington starts with LaVou, Markson, and Kingcade with Bowman and Lyle on defense. Line-ups are flowing across the top of your screen courtesy of Truman Paint and Lumber, your premier paint supplier in the greater Harrisburg area. Lockhart picks up the puck and carries it down to the Washington end."

"Lockhart has looked much better the second half of this season. Coming back from that shoulder surgery was a long haul but his play has improved tremendously. He's now second in goals and assists on the Railers, right behind Tennant Rowe."

"It's hard for anyone to get past Tennant Rowe on those stat sheets, Heller. A solid shot on the Washington net sees the shot go up and out of play."

"Man alive, did he ever wind that baby up. He just got a little tight on his skate there as he took the shot."

"Both teams are quick on making substitutions tonight as some line juggling takes place to try to counter the strengths on the other team as play is about to resume."

"I'm not sure Washington has a strong enough roster to counter the Railers first line, Dusky."

"I guess we'll see as the game goes on. Washington wins that faceoff, and they carry it down into the Railers end with speed. Maybe their coach lit a fire under them during intermission, Heller."

"Hey, could be, I know my backside was charbroiled many a time when I was playing."

"Williams dishes off to Prescott as they break into the Railers zone. Fetcher moves in for a scorching shot that Lyamin has to stretch to block, the shot going up into the netting to stop play yet again."

"Lyamin is not getting up, Dusky. He's still face down on the ice. That didn't look like that hard of a move for the Railers goalie to make. Play is called as the Railers trainer heads onto the ice. Dang, you hate to see this. Lyamin is still down on the ice, his teammates gathered close to the crease as Paul Iman, the Railers head trainer for the past few years, tends to the net minder."

"Let's see a replay of that shot from Prescott and maybe we can see...Oh, oh, okay, see that extension

Lyamin makes to move from the left of his crease to the right? I'm wondering if he didn't pull another groin muscle on that move, Heller."

"Hmm, could be, Dusky. The butterfly technique that so many of today's goalies use transfers some big pressure to the hip joints. Hopefully it's just a tweak and—"

"Looks like Bryan Delaney is gearing up. That is not good news for the Railers. I'd personally like to see Lyamin get to his skates and leave the ice on his own volition but he's still not moving much other than his head, which is now free of his famed Elvis mask, and his hands. He seems to be in some real pain."

"Yeah, they're calling for the stretcher for him. Lyamin is the spirit of this team while Rowe is the heart. Let's hope the problem is a minor one for our beloved goalie…"

Chapter One

STAN

"… only for the labral tear we'd be looking at two to six months until you could possibly return to play, but since there is also the issue of the osteoarthritis that has led to the worn sockets on both hips that *still* require replacement surgery, my personal opinion as your orthopedic surgeon is to get both replacements done now."

I looked down at my feet under the stiff white hospital sheets. "How long?"

When no one replied, I glanced at my surgeon, a tall Indian man with a long nose and the kindest eyes. Erik stood beside my bed, his curls tighter than usual as he had rushed to the hospital near the barn to be here all night at my side and had not used conditioner as he normally did. The pain in my right hip was manageable. Just. The pain in the left one was the ache I had been pushing through for two years now. Bone grinding on bone hurts bigly.

Dr. Mehta folded his arms over his chest, his white coat bright in the morning sun streaming through my hospital room window.

"Are you asking how long until you can walk after the surgery, or are you asking how soon you can play after the surgery?" Dr. Mehta enquired as if he didn't already know which question I wished to have answered first. I was an athlete.

"How long until I can play again?" I clarified, my husband making a small sound of dislike I ignored for now. I knew how Erik felt about my bad hips. He had mentioned me hanging up my skates more than once. My left shoulder also had arthritis in it, as did my left hand. Mama said I got it from her side of the family. Her toes hurt when the barometer dropped so it could be I did inherit it from her.

"I would not recommend returning to the ice before a full year was up, and that would be after you were cleared by a few physical therapists, the team, and of course, me."

"A year," I whispered as a melancholy began to settle in my chest. A year was a long time for a player to be out. Bryan would take over, admirably, as he had last night to get my team the win. I admired Bryan greatly, but I did not want him to take my place. "That is a long time."

"It will fly by, honey," Erik said, reaching out to clasp my hand. My doctor nodded. As if I didn't know they were trying to make me feel better.

"I am sure you are puffing smoke up my rectum," I muttered, tried to shift off my ass bone, and nearly blacked out from the pain in my hip joint.

My doctor moved to the bed, adjusted something on my IV, and then placed his skilled hand on my shoulder—the one that ached when it was cold or when a rainstorm was coming in. Truly, I was becoming my mother more and more every day. Next I would be seen sweeping the front lawn while wearing a headscarf.

"Stan, it's time. You've put this surgery off for years. We've done everything that we could short of replacing the joints, but now with this tear…"

He let it hang. Which was fine, I was in too much pain for him to go on harping about my hips and the damage I was doing to my body. How walking oddly was impacting my spine and lower back. I knew all of this. It was me who had to sleep with a pillow between my thighs to get any rest at night. I was aware of the toll my body was suffering through so I could continue to compete.

"Stan, I'll be with you through it all," Erik said, his bright blue eyes damp with concern. "The kids, Mama, your sister, we'll all help you recover."

I nodded. "I know this to be true. I just worry that when I leave, I will never go back." I had seen many a great goalie have to step aside, most around my age, and it scared me to death. The thought of surgery or the pain of the rehab did not frighten me, it was the notion of being cast aside like a suitcase that had seen thousands of miles of travel being placed at the curb because it had lost a wheel.

"Would it be all that bad, Stan, really?" Erik asked softly.

He spoke out of worry. My husband was a hockey player as well, his whole life dedicated to our sport, and he too knew that leaving that sport would be a huge loss of self. If I am not the Railers starting goalie, then who am I?

I didn't answer my sweet one. Instead, I closed my eyes, the agony in my hip easing, and then I let my head fall back to the pillows piled up behind me.

"I will have the surgery," I said on a breath out.

I heard Erik exhale, the words "Thank God" rushing out of him, as he held my hand even tighter.

"It will all work out," Erik whispered then lifted my knuckles to his lips.

I was not so sure how things would work out. My achy shoulder was telling me that stormy times were ahead, times that had little to do with the weather.

Chapter Two

My heart ached as I sat beside Stan's hospital bed, the faint hum of the hospital equipment a backdrop to my fears, as I stared at the man I loved so much. My vibrant, always-on-the-move husband looked small and fragile against the crisp hospital sheets, and the sterile white of the room seemed to make Stan's skin appear even paler and showed the flecks of white starting to appear at his temples. He moaned about going gray, that he was only thirty-nine, that Elvis never went gray, but he backed down when I'd explained in no uncertain terms how sexy he was. Stan that was, not Elvis.

"Elvis is sexy," Stan had argued.

So, I'd shut him up by kissing him and he'd backed down after the second orgasm.

That was the day before we'd met the doctor, only a week ago, and he was here, away from playing, away from his family, and not curled up beside me in our bed.

I couldn't even stay—the Railers were playing game three against a feisty Washington team tonight —and given it was a home game in our barn, I'd said I could still play.

I didn't want to.

Stan made me do it.

I legit hated him for it, for about five minutes, and then he told me I had to win the Stanley Cup for him. As if that would make everything better.

"I hate this," I murmured, echoing the sentiment I'd expressed countless times in the hour I'd been waiting for him to wake. The deep lines of pain that I was the only one to see, that had marked his face for weeks now were absent in his medicated sleep, and while I watched Stan's steady breathing, I could almost imagine he was okay. I hated that he had been in such pain, that my stubborn husband had put off surgery and hidden the worst of his suffering from the world, but what I hated the most was knowing he had faced the operating theater alone.

We were never apart.

From raising our family to playing hockey, we did

everything side by side. Yet, today, I had to watch from the sidelines.

People talked about Ten, about how he was the face of the team, but Stan—my Stan—had been their backstop, the defensive wall, the final no to so many shots on goal. He'd won games for us, way before Ten was drafted. Bryan was talented, but he wasn't Stan. Not yet. Would he rise to the challenge of being the starting goalie, hell, would he survive an entire post-season if the Railers went the whole way? I groaned and rubbed my eyes, the insistent thought that maybe I didn't want the Railers to go the whole way when what I really wanted was to be by Stan's side?

Traitor. Stan would kill me.

Hockey was more than just a game for him—it was part of his makeup. But that deep-seated passion came at a cost, and now here he was, post-operation, looking at an apparently endless recovery period. A whole year? How could he handle being away from the game for so long?

Anxiety and regret gnawed at me. Had I pushed too hard for this surgery? Had I been too insistent this was the journey he should be taking right now? I wanted nothing more than for Stan to live without pain, but had an operation been the right solution?

"Please don't resent me!" I blurted, but he didn't stir. Shit, I was talking to an empty room; but he needed to hear. "I did this for you, I want you to heal, I want to walk along a beach, hand in hand in our seventies, with our grandkids…" I stopped, because the visceral need for Stan to be by my side in all of these things was overwhelming.

The thought of him resenting me was unbearable.

I thought of our family, how our lives revolved around hockey. Noah, our twelve-year-old, was already carving a path for himself in the sport, attending hockey camp in the break, not a defenseman like me, nor a goalie like Stan, but a fast and spiky center man with potential. It wasn't just me who could sense the generational handover of our family's hockey legacy—Stan had said the same thing, but then… when he said it, he'd been sad, regretful.

He wasn't ready to let go.

Taking a deep breath, I leaned in, whispering to my still sleeping husband, "Wake up, baby."

A nurse came in, startling me from watching him. She checked his vitals, nodding and smiling at me, "Not long now, Mr. Gunnerson-Lyamin, and he'll be awake."

"Call me Erik, please, and you're sure? Yes?"

"Erik, then." She patted my arm as she passed me.

"This is Stan we're talking about." As if that made a difference. Everyone imagined him as this indestructible man, but I'd seen him crumble, and cry, and have pain no one else saw.

I *knew* him.

"Thank you."

It wasn't long after she'd poked at him that a slight movement from the bed caught my attention. Stan's eyelids fluttered, his eyes initially glazed and unfocused. I went to his side, searching for pain in his beautiful gray eyes, and at first he smiled, and then as clarity returned, a touch of uncharacteristic grumpiness surfaced as he growled for water. I darted out for ice chips and to tell the nurse he was awake, and then hurried back in, pressed a kiss to his forehead—he was hot, so I helped him with ice chips. The nurse came back, carried out a few more perfunctory checks and then she left after suggesting he'd be disoriented and that I should delay the entire family visiting for at least another hour or so. I sent a quick message to Eva, who was down in the hospital restaurant corralling Margo, Noah, and Stan's momma, saying all was okay, and received a heart emoji in return.

I offered a hesitant smile to Stan who turned his head to look at me, whispering, "Hey."

Stan tried to reply, but it was a soft *"hey."* I knew him so well that as he oriented himself, I saw the weight of the surgery's reality settle in.

"Everything's okay," I began, leaning over the bed to cradle his face, pressing another kiss to his forehead, seeing the confusion in him, and reassuring him as best I could. "Surgery went well, baby, it's all good. Okay?"

He closed his eyes, nodded, winced, and reached for my hand.

And all I could do was hold it and reassure him in gentle words that I was here, and that he'd be okay, and that he'd heal quickly and be back on the ice in no time.

I lied about the last part.

He closed his eyes, I think he even slept, but after an hour, when I could hold it off no longer, Momma brought the kids up with her. They flocked to Stan's side, careful not to disturb him too much. Noah was in full Railers kit, same as Eva who was leaving for college in the fall. Margo was sunshine, beautiful in a long, flowing summer dress. All of them had brought small gifts they'd made while waiting in the family room. And while Stan wrapped his arms around them, wincing when they knocked him, I noticed a somberness, a deep loss in his gaze. It was the look of someone grappling with a life-altering shift, and I hoped the kids didn't pick up on it.

Given there were no complications during or, thank goodness, after the surgery, there was no need for an extended hospital stay, and on day three, just when we'd reached peak grumpy-Stan, he was allowed to go home with a whole list of warnings, and after lengthy discussions with the Railers rehab team. Movement would be limited for a while, and twisting and pivoting was out of the realms of possibility.

For the first time since that meeting in the doctor's office, Stan showed his humorous side. "My hip-shaking hunka-hunka move is off the limits for a little bits."

I was so relieved, I could have cried, which was freaking ridiculous.

So, today was the great escape day, and as the hospital doors slid open, I found myself preparing for the challenge that lay ahead. Stan, ever the stubborn one, had a frown that could rival a thunderstorm, and I couldn't blame him.

"Stupid not walking," he grumbled, "I'm bigly walking fine."

"Yeah? No," was all I said, and I sighed, doing

my best to keep my tone patient. "It's just hospital protocol, Stan. Plus, we don't want to risk any complications. It's only for a short while, okay?"

He grunted in response, clearly not convinced. I couldn't help but smile, remembering why I had fallen in love with this fiercely independent—stubbornly idiotic—man. I bet if Stan could've willed it, he'd be shimmying out of the hospital without a care in the world. As we made our way to the car, I kept the conversation light, trying to distract him from his current predicament.

"The kids have planned something special for you at home," I hinted.

He gave me a smile and raised an eyebrow. "What kind of something?"

"You'll see."

"Mama cooking all the things?"

"All the things," I said, recalling the scents of peppers and mustard filling our huge house as I'd left. Not to mention the banners, and the lights, and the…

Yeah, I'd just let the kids get on with it, and when Ten had gotten involved I knew it would be okay. Over-the-top, probably, but then Stan deserved it—anything to make him smile.

We entered the house, after a lot of cursing, with Stan suggesting that pain could go fuck itself at least twice, in Russian, which unfortunately for him I understood completely. As soon as we stepped inside, Elvis's "Jailhouse Rock" filled the air and I blinked at the bright in-your-face chaos of it all. In the three hours I'd been gone, the front room and hallway had been transformed into an Elvis-themed wonderland with records, posters, and everyone wearing quirky Elvis wigs. Ten and Jared were there, along with Adler and Layton, plus Bryan and his partner, Gatlin. It was a party.

Maybe it was too much?

Or maybe I should stop thinking of Stan as being an invalid and hope his grumpiness slid away and the pain wasn't too bad.

"Welcome home, Graceland style!" Ten declared, ever the enthusiastic one, doing his best Elvis impersonation.

Jared, in contrast, gave Stan a serious nod, his way of showing concern without drowning in Elvis-themed happiness. "Glad to have you back, man."

Adler turned to show the huge Elvis face on his shirt, Stan's mama turned to reveal a matching one, and the kids broke out into some kind of choreographed dance.

Stan tapped his fingers on the wheelchair in time

to the song, grinning, the tension in his face easing a little as the song drew to an end.

"Is most good show. Like Las Vegas without girls in feathers," he said before we hoisted him to his feet for the arduous move from wheelchair to recliner. His face pinched with pain at each step. Thank God there were only a few.

The aroma of delicious food wafted from the kitchen, and I could see an array of soft drinks set out on the table. Everyone was trying to keep the atmosphere light and fun, and for a moment, Stan looked happy.

Bryan approached, his expression holding a mix of relief and concern. "Good to see you out of there, Stan. We missed you at game four."

Stan's eyes lit up. Hockey. "Good winning!" he exclaimed, then frowned.

I could see his mind churning out things to say about the fact the Railers were tied two games each, or that Bryan needed to fix this, or that, between the pipes—I cut him off with a deliberate kiss, and after a moment of surprise he melted into the embrace.

"Break it up, boys, we have food!" Adler exclaimed.

"Tell me the hockey!" Stan said loudly as soon as

our kiss ended, as if he'd been biding his time to say the words.

Bryan hesitated, glancing my way, as if seeking permission. Hockey could well be a touchy subject right now, given everything. But seeing Stan's eager face, I gave a nod, signaling it was okay, but I hoped the warning with it—ignore his grumpiness over not playing—came over strong.

Bryan grinned. "We nailed game four. Won comfortably."

"Bryan was a genius in net," Adler announced, and Layton shoved him at his lack of tact, but that was typical Adler. "What did I say?" he defended as Layton rolled his eyes.

But Stan was chuckling, and his face lit up. "Tell me all the things!" he demanded.

As the hour wore on, Stan tried his best to stay engaged and upbeat, even with the pain and discomfort. Every now and then, I'd catch him grimacing or shifting in his seat. But he soldiered on, for the sake of our kids, our friends, and for himself, and reminded me of the strength and resilience of my man I had chosen to spend my life with.

Despite the challenges that lay ahead, everything would be okay.

Right?

Chapter Three

STAN

I have suffered through many embarrassing things in my life.

There was the one time as a young man I fell out of a boat into an icy pond. Oh, how my friends laughed as I battled to get to shore wound up in fishing line and bobbers.

There was that night that I was playing *Pokéman Go* with Tennant and walked into a streetlight as I chased down a Shiny Spinda. Tennant nearly wet his pants he laughed so hard.

Then there was that time I tripped over my feet while performing/lip-syncing "My Way" sung by Elvis for all my guests at last year's Elvis' Birthday Jamboree party at my home. I fell on an inflatable hockey stick of Noah's and the noise that erupted from the blow-up stick as it ruptured sounded just like a massive fart. Everyone in attendance roared as I sat there blushing with a flat stick between my legs.

None of the above came close to the humiliation of having to have my mother help me into the shower so I could wash my ass. I'd just had my stitches out and was in dire need of a scrubbing. You do not realize just how wondrous a thing a shower is until you cannot have one.

Mama had been a marvelous nurse while Erik was traveling, patient and kind, firm though, not allowing me to sit for longer than I should. Nudging me to walk as the doctors said I must even though it pained me terribly to get up out of the chair. Nothing hurt worse than exiting a car, though. For some reason when I had moved to lower my leg getting out at the surgeon's office earlier it had hurt so bad I was close to crying. Although my physical therapy came a very close second to getting out of the car.

Now, here I was, a man of near forty, having his mother steady him as he stepped into the shower.

"Perhaps we both will need walk-in baths soon, Mama," I ground out in Russian as she steadied me, my backside exposed to the world as my robe fell off my shoulders. Using my hand to steady myself, palms to the walls, so I didn't slip and fall—I could not imagine the agony of having to go through all of this again because I'd tumbled to the floor and broken something in one of my new hips—I eased my left leg over the side and had to stop to catch my breath.

"Stan, you should have let me bring my shower chair into your bathroom," she scolded gently as I grumbled and winced. Perhaps I should have but that was just… no. I'd use a walker, crutches, and a cane. I would use those pincher things to pick up something I'd dropped. I would even use an elevated toilet seat. But having a chair in my shower was just a step too far for my pride to bear. I had to cling to some shred of manliness. Panting after stepping into a tub was a slap in the face.

Me, a professional athlete, had to pause after taking one step. It was humiliating and depressing, and yes, infuriating. I could barely turn on the taps to start my shower without cussing at the pull on my hips. My ego was displeased with everyone waiting on me.

"Perhaps so. Easy now, Stanislav, do not overdo," she warned, turning from me with her hand out. I eased my robe the rest of the way off, handed it to her, and then closed the shower curtain. "Stand still in there." What did she think I was going to do? Dance the Lezginka? "I will wait out here until you are done."

I grunted as I eased myself under the stream. Never had hot water felt so good. I stood there for the longest time just letting the jets pulse on my face, trying not to think too far ahead. Live in the moment as they say. Worrying over the rest of my therapy would only rob me of this tiny moment of accomplishment and joy. Silly to be proud of such a small thing but after surgery even the tiniest success —like being able to stand with the aid of a walker and use the bathroom instead of pissing into a portable urinal—was a major deal. A huge deal as my husband had beamed at me when I'd first peed by myself. How I wished Erik were here now, but he was off playing hockey. My team had moved onto the next round of the playoffs and were now down in Florida facing off against Tennant's brother and his team. The Railers were in yet another game seven and here I sat, like a bumpy toad on a log, having my mother tend to me since I had refused home nursing.

It was bad enough to have my family see me tottering around like an old man. I would be double damned, as Jared would say, to allow a stranger to come in and see me like this. Yes, I knew that pride landed before destruction. My spouse had informed me of that Biblical quote when I had declined any help outside family. He had not been happy. His brow had furrowed, and his kissable lips had flattened. It was a good look for him, but I declined to mention that as he muttered under his breath about hard-headed men. I had asked if that meant he was a soft-hearted man as per the wonderful Elvis song. He had not been amused and had glowered at me as he packed his bags to leave for an away game.

And here I stood, my biggest feat of the day, taking a shower.

"Are you okay?" Mama called in our native tongue.

I sighed, licked the water off my lips, and let my eyes drift shut. Knowing she would open the curtain if she felt I was in any distress—Mama was a wonderful but worrisome nurse—I reached for the shampoo and began washing my gritty hair. It felt wonderful. Standing for so long was making my new hips ache but they always ached. Although, I must confess, the pain was different than what I'd been living with for so long so that was a good sign. Or so Lance, the sadist at PT, had told me.

"Da, Mama, I am good. I will linger for a bit."

"Okay, I am running to check the stew."

I heard the door close. I rinsed my hair then

lathered up my soap, scrubbing merrily, each pass of that bar of soap lifting some of the funk.

"Dad?" Noah called.

Surely with four baths a man could find some peace to bathe, yes?

"Yes, Son, what is it?" I called as I lathered up the back scrubber once more. The smell of a Celtic forest refilled the shower, adding to my uplifted emotions. I was doing well today. Yes, they were small steps, but they were steps.

"Can I fill my water bottle up in here? Eva and Margo are using the other bathrooms, and Grandma has her pantyhose drying in hers and you know…"

I smiled to myself. It wasn't right for a boy his age to see bloomers and big brassieres his granny wore up close and personal. And yes, he used those terms. Our son was quite the character. And yes, he was right.

"Yes, Noah, I know." I eased back a step and then two, taking care to ensure my big, doofy feet were on the mat. "Didn't you just fill up that bottle before I came up the stairs?"

"Yeah, I get thirsty."

"You don't drink enough during practices," I answered, got a half-hearted "Okay, Dad," and then felt a chilly draft blowing around the shower curtain.

Noah had left the door open. Again. The corner of the shower curtain moved. A big black nose pushed it aside and King, the latest addition to our pack, shoved his massive brown head into the shower. The mutt—all of our dogs were rescues from the shelter Ben and Max ran—began licking the puddles on the wall. Another dog entered, then another, and then one of the two cats that had claimed us in the past year arrived and began batting at the curtain, claws out, to ruck it aside for a peek at my bare bottom.

"Can someone please to shut the door?" I yelled but only got a happy woof and a plaintive meow in reply. I blew out a breath, rinsed my backside, and began spritzing the dogs with water. They loved it. The cat? No so much.

Mama arrived then, got a face-full of water, and chided me for acting like one of the children while shooing the dogs out of the bathroom. I laughed, maybe for the first time since I had gone under the knife, and it felt good. Damn good.

What did not feel good was mini squats.

Nope, did not like. Lance, the smiling twink with two earrings and no soul, stood beside me as I lowered myself, gripping a bar on the wall at the PT center in the newly built Greater Harrisburg Sports Rehab Complex. The massive building sat one block away from the arena and was where all the Railers went for physical therapy after injuries or surgeries.

"You're doing really well, Stan, just a few more reps, then we'll get you on the treadmill. How did you feel during the one-leg-stand-ball-catch sequence?"

I straightened, took a sip of water, and then turned to face my tormentor. Lance was not there to hurt me, this I knew, and he was working hard to get me through rehab so I could return to the ice.

"Okay, is good for balance work." He smiled as if I had handed him a bag of money. "I know is a long time for me to play but if you had to guess…"

I let that dangle. He ran a hand through his bright yellow hair. "I know you are not happy to make guesses for times. But I am doing well, yes?"

"Yes, you're doing quite well. Let's move to the treadmill now." He walked beside me, one hand on my lower back, as I shuffled past the bikes, which I had done upon arrival, then around a set of steps an old man in a knee brace was climbing gingerly with help from a young woman named Kim who had two Dalmatians, so we talked dogs when Lance was not working me like a taskmaster. A good taskmaster, yes, but still a taskmaster.

"I take note of you not answering me," I said while inch by inch lifting one foot then the other up on to the treadmill.

"You're right, I didn't reply. Stan, yes, you are doing incredibly well. But I don't want to set any definitive dates for your return to play as there are so many variables. Why don't we take things week by week as we agreed the last time you were here."

"Fine, yes, I know I say good to weekly but weekly is slow and making me grumpy."

He chuckled then tapped in a creeping speed for me to walk. "I've dealt with grumpy athletes before. One of the college footballers threatened to punt me through the goal posts if I didn't work him harder than guidelines dictate. I told him to go ahead and boot me through the uprights if he could catch me."

"Ah, so he was having a bad knee?"

"*Terrible* knee injury. But we got him back on the field for the next season and I am glad to say no punting of the therapist took place." He patted my forearm. "Stay at this speed for the next fifteen minutes. Then we'll get you onto a table for some heat therapy."

Ah yes, I did enjoy the heat therapy. Also, the

massages. "I will walk. And I will not threaten you with kicking through posts."

"It's greatly appreciated," he joked then moved off to supervise my walk as he tended to some work on his tablet. Probably he was jotting down notes on my progress, which would be fed to the team as they were, I was hoping, still interested in how I was coming along. Not that they needed me in the net. Bryan had taken over, been a brick wall in goal, steady on his skates, cool under pressure, and given to small celebrations after a win. The Railers had called up a young tendie from Colchester by the name of Brigham Travis, an amazing young goalie who had led the Colts to a championship victory last season. Neither of them spoke to the pipes. I wondered if they missed me, my hometown pipes. I bet they did. If I got back in net—no, not if *when*—I could catch them up. If I did not they would not grant me good luck as they had for so many years.

Lost in my thoughts as I was, the walk ended soon, and I was then given a lovely massage that left me rubbery and sleepy. I was not driving. Eva had agreed to pick me up after gathering her brother and sister from their various practices. Noah was in a summer league now and Margo was playing soccer. We'd come to rely on our eldest daughter for so much in terms of helping with the younger children that when she left in the fall for her first year of college down in West Virginia we'd be lost. But she had dreams of being a child psychologist, and she was eighteen now, so we had to let her go. Not that Erik and I were close to being mentally ready to do so. To us she would always be that thin, haunted child we'd brought home from Russia.

My eldest child was waiting outside the rehab center when I shuffled out. She opened the car door for me, Margo, and Noah in the back of the SUV, watching me as if they were scared I might fall over at any moment.

"Papa, you're walking so much better every day," Eva said, tossing her dark, waist-length hair over her shoulder to catch the eye of several young men lingering outside as they waited for their appointments. I glowered at the pack of wolves. Each one was quick to find something interesting on their phones. "Next week you'll be jogging."

"From your mouth to the gods' ears," I replied as I eased myself into the seat, grateful for this higher vehicle than Mama's lower car. I glanced in the back while Eva toted my crutches to the rear of the car to stow them with Noah's hockey equipment and Margo's bag of soccer gear.

"Papa, today I ran the fastest in warm-ups and got this cool sticker." Margo beamed at me as she pointed at the bright pink sticker on her striped gold and blue T-shirt. We'd been thrilled to find a camp that was inclusive and didn't balk at letting our trans child play in the girls' squads. It had been a depressing slog to find a camp that did not wish to slap her into the boys' squads based on her gender at birth. After we'd been welcomed, several of the Railers had made generous donations to the camp, Erik and I included, to show financial support so such welcoming places could continue to function.

"That is good, pumpkin," I said with a smile then glanced at Noah who was dozing, his head resting on the window to his left.

Eva slid behind the wheel, looked into the back, and sighed. "He really needs to go to bed earlier, Papa. Perhaps you need to flip the switch on his PS5 at ten o'clock instead of eleven."

I stared at our son as he slumbered. Perhaps we did. Noah was always such a ball of energy but if his obsession with a certain fantasy video game was tiring him out so much I might have to intervene. I'd see how he did over the next week or so.

"I will keep watch," I told Eva, who nodded then pointed at my seatbelt. I hurried to buckle up after I got my two new hips settled under me. "You are such a mother hen," I teased my daughter and got a cluck in reply.

Margo giggled. Noah snored. I sighed as the heated seat warmed my butt, the heat spreading into my lower back perfectly. My eyes were heavy as well. Perhaps Eva would have to rouse both the weary Lyamin men in this car when we got home.

A heavy metal song blared from the stereo, startling me from my PT-induced lethargy.

Okay, so perhaps she would *not* have to rouse me from a nap after all.

Chapter Four

ERIK

We always knew that Toronto would be coming in hot, after winning both of their matchups four games to nothing. Where we'd had to fight past Washington and Florida, taking each matchup to the full seven games, they'd had it easy.

Well, as easy as it gets playing hockey.

Easier than us at least.

They would be fresh, and playing in their barn for games one and two out of the possible seven we'd need to play gave them home town advantage. The roar of the home crowd was deafening, echoing throughout the heart of the arena and I could feel the weight of the thousands of eyes on us, the hope and expectation of Toronto's loyal fans palpable in the air. It had been a long time since they'd showed so much promise in the post season, and the fan support was a force of its own, giving their team a boost that I knew we'd have to constantly battle against.

Eyes on the prize.

Skating onto the ice for the game, I loved the sting of the cold that hit my face. I ignored the burn in my muscles, the fatigue threatening to pull me down. We were all tired, every one of the Railers. It had been a long season, a grueling set of games leading to this point. But none of that mattered now.

I glanced over at Bryan roughing the ice in front of goal, his eyes focused, a steely determination as he muttered to himself. I knew he felt the weight of replacing Stan, and much as I wished Stan was healthy and standing there talking to his pipes, I knew Bryan had our backs. The first line was out, Ten taking the face-off against a determined Andre Cristo, Toronto's captain, the puck dropped, and everything else vanished. The game was on.

The first few minutes were chaos, Toronto pushing, us protecting, then the Railers getting the edge, only for Toronto to block anything we tried to make. A tap on my shoulder indicated it was our line-up, the fourth line, keeping the game moving. I fell into my right wing position as easily as breathing, Charlie at center, and Brookes, the new kid pulled up from the minors, who retained that wonder of all things Stanley Cup, on left wing. I never felt more like a veteran than when the kid playing on my line was just nineteen. He could skate rings around us when it came to speed, but he lacked the experience, and the muscle memory of me and Charlie who had several seasons between us.

My blades bit into the ice, each stride was driven by pure adrenaline, and me ignoring every ache in my body. We had a couple of good chances, darting between Toronto's defense, trying to find a gap, a moment of weakness we could make work for us.

Toronto was not making it easy. Their defense was ironclad, their forwards swift and dangerous. Several times, I found myself up against their enforcer, Oskar Venti, a mountain of a man who wasn't shy about throwing his weight around. This time, I had the puck, stole it from his defense partner, swung to start a charge, the puck leaving my stick as I shuffled it across to Brookes, the damn thing wobbling as Venti slammed into me with a heavy check, sending me sprawling onto the ice. The hit was clean but hard, a clear message—they weren't going to give an inch.

Regaining my footing, shaky, aching, I managed to intercept a pass, sending it up the ice to Brookes who'd somehow managed to find space. He deked past one defenseman, then sent a quick pass to Charlie in the slot. I could see the opportunity, the Toronto net minder out of position, thrown off maybe by the hit to me, imagining that was our push done.

Charlie's shot deflected off a Toronto player, and I found myself in the perfect position to grab the loose puck, Venti a hair's breadth behind me, almost as if I could feel him reaching for me. With the goalie scrambling to reset, I took my shot, sending the puck rocketing towards the top corner.

The arena went silent for a split second, and then there was a sound that will forever be etched into my memory: the soft thud of the puck hitting the back of the net. The Railers' bench erupted in joy, and I was swamped by my teammates.

Despite our fatigue, despite being the away team, we had taken a goal in the fourth minute of the game.

I was alive. I was like the king of all hockey, this was everything to me, the roar of our fans, the boos of our opposition's fans, the ice, the cold, the love, and congratulations directed at me. It didn't matter than my shin hurt like fuck. I could ignore that maybe there was damage to this old, tired body from the hit.

This was why I played. For the group. For the team. For this one shining moment.

Only, it was momentary, a few seconds in a game of attrition we lost by three goals, my puck in the net the single goal the Railers had managed. Toronto had smothered Ten, kept his skills in check and when we skated off the ice, we were spent, and it didn't matter how many sports psychologists we would see, every one of us, at the back of our minds, accepted this might well be Toronto's year. This was just game one, the series was far from over, but somehow the battles were getting too hard to win.

What if the Railers had a team filled with the new kids, the fast ones, the ones who'd come up through so much training they hit the ice the first time and scored goals.

Was there room for me on this team?

"Tough game," Ten said as he slumped into the cubby opposite mine. Several players made noises of agreement. "We'll get them next time," he added. I know he was trying to make things right, but if Tennant Rowe, phenom, couldn't get free of Toronto's D-men, then what were the rest of us going to do?

That wasn't fair.

That almost sounded as though I were trying to

blame Ten. I wasn't. This wasn't all on him. We were outmatched.

And worse, we were up in Toronto, in hotel rooms, and Stan was down in Harrisburg, and I freaking missed him like nothing I'd ever felt before.

It was a dull ache that matched the pain in my shin.

We had a day to rest after the game, and I pretended not to hobble down to breakfast, but clearly, I didn't do a good enough job, Coach pulling me to one side.

"See the PT," he ordered, without explanation or question.

I'd done all the post-game cooldowns last night, stretched out the pain, iced, taken an anti-inflammatory, but I was way too experienced not to understand what was happening to me.

Every shift felt as If I'd taken a puck to the outside left shin, and it didn't subside until I sat on the bench and rested. Right shin too but thank fuck that hurt much less. What worried me most was that my ankle rotation was limited, because the muscle was cramped and fatigued, and I couldn't get on the proper edge without a lot of opposing effort. I knew what I was doing.

A PT didn't have to check my range of motion for me to know that.

Ice, meds, foam rolling, compression sleeves, rest —that was all Toby gave me as he frowned and pushed and pulled and made my life fucking uncomfortable.

"You know what I'm going to add," he began after listing all the things I needed to do and sighed. "Erik…" He didn't even speak the rest, used to us idiot players demanding to play through even the worst pain.

I mean look at Stan, hell, the pain he must have been in, yet game after game he'd chased that high of stopping goals, of winning, of bringing the team home to victory. He was a warrior. We all were.

But even warriors have their time.

Game two wasn't any better, Ten scored twice in the first ten minutes, and for a while there was hope that maybe the first game against them had been a fluke, and that the mighty Railers, two-time Stanley Cup champions, would fight back.

And then it collapsed.

We lost five–two, never capitalizing on that initial push.

And the pain in my shins, the burning in my chest, missing Stan so bad it hurt…

It was all too much.

He was waiting for me at the airport when we got off the plane, and I knew he'd be grumpy that he couldn't get out of the car, Eva was standing in front of the SUV grinning. I was behind Bryan walking down the stairs, dejection rolling off the kid in waves.

I nudged him. "Go talk to Stan first."

He turned to me, to ask me if I was sure, but then said nothing, and almost sprinted across the tarmac to get to the car. I slowed my roll, but as I got closer, I could see Stan's hand on Bryan's shoulder, probably imparting wisdom that came from all his years of experience. Bryan was backstopping the entire team, and the pressure was his alone with Stan here at home. I stopped a short distance away, giving them time to talk, and Eva ran to me. I picked her up and swung her in my arms, setting her down and hugging her.

"Papa's not doing so well," she murmured in my ear.

She didn't have to say anymore. I knew my husband—he'd be tired, and irritable, and frustrated he couldn't play. I pushed aside the losses, and the shin issues, and the exhaustion, and pasted the biggest damn smile on my face as Eva and I sauntered the final distance. Bryan jumped up from where he'd been crouching next to Stan, and he fist-bumped me, gave Eva a quick hug, and then jogged to where I could see Gatlin parked. I waved at the tattoo artist, who returned the greeting, and then it was my turn to face Stan.

"Babe," he said in his most gentle tone.

I leaned into the passenger seat and melted into his hold. The scent of him surrounded me, the warmth of him was everything I needed. He held me so tight and so close I wanted to stay there forever. Which, yeah, impractical, but still, I wasn't letting him go for a while.

I kissed him, maybe a little desperately.

He cradled my face and eased me away. "What's wrong?" Stan asked, his soft growly voice smooth and sweet.

"You mean besides losing and me feeling like I'm too old for this shit?" I deadpanned.

He stroked away one of the curls that fell over my eyes, "Something else," he said, and gave me a quick kiss.

He could see right through me, to the indecision and sadness underneath. The question about who I was without hockey had the best answer—I was a husband, a son, a father. I was loved, and it was everything. I couldn't say the words though, I couldn't admit out loud I was tired, and maybe it was time for me to retire, not when Stan was fighting so hard to get back to what he loved. I had to be strong for him as he healed.

Maybe everything would feel better if he'd been in Toronto with me?

But that would mean him playing through pain, through disabling himself by pushing too hard, and maybe ruining his life.

So why was I staying quiet?

When we got home, I had commiscrating hugs from everyone, including all the dogs and none of the cats, lots of food from Stan's mama, which fixed everything in her world. Noah seemed low, but then he was a huge Railers fan. His hope was that one day he'd play for the team, and he hated that we'd lost. He went to bed early, juggling two water bottles, and even though he hugged me goodnight, there nothing I could say that seemed to cheer him up.

Hockey was his life, as much as it was mine and Stan's.

When Stan and I made it to bed, and he was medicated and comfortable in his nest of pillows to support the part that hurt, and other parts that were healing, I snuggled close to him and kissed his shoulder, lying there in silence and thinking through everything that had happened, with so much I wanted to tell him.

It wouldn't hurt to tell him that I missed him, right? That I had so much of the world to see, and that I wanted him to be whole and healthy next to me.

"I want to see Rome one day," I blurted. "Take the whole family. All of us. To Florence. I want to see Michelangelo's David. And I want to go to Paris and see the Eiffel Tower, London… I've always wanted to go to London. I don't want to do it alone. I don't like being alone. I missed you so badly."

But he didn't hear any of it because he'd fallen asleep.

Chapter Five

STAN

Even after all of our years together I never tired of waking up beside Erik.

Spending so much time apart had hammered in the knowledge that this man was my everything. So, as the sun peeked through the thin slats on our bedroom window, I reached out to my side, seeking his body. He was on the very edge of the bed. Rolling my head in his direction, I took just a few precious moments—in a house filled with children and pets, time alone to admire the curve of your husband's firm biceps was rare—and just drank him in. My gaze moved over his curls, glowing deep gold in the early rays of a summer day, his long neck, the lines of his shoulder exposed to the warm summer air. I studied the thin line of a scar by his shoulder blade. The slim white mark left from a blade many years ago during a childhood shinny game. My fingers danced over his hip, over the soft cotton of his sleep shorts, on a mission to find his sleepy prick nestled all comfy in a bed of soft blond curls. What I wouldn't give to be able to shift to my side, wiggle his shorts down, and slide my cock into his warm, waiting body. But those kinds of maneuvers were in the distant future. Thankfully there were other ways to make each other happy.

My dick, which was already awake, liked that thought a great deal. I was pleased to note now the pain had eased off; my libido had made a recovery of its own. If only I could get up off my back. Erik snuffled awake as my pinkie brushed the tip of his cock. With a jolt he was up, off the bed, curls riotous around his head, staring at me with wide, sleepy, sky blue eyes.

"What are you doing?" he barked as he shoved at his half-hard shaft. "You just had surgery. There is no way you're up for sex." He threw the covers back, took hold of my rigid cock, and gave it a shake. His eye roll made me smile. "Okay, fine, *that* part of you is up for sex. Your new hips aren't."

"Then we won't use my new hips. See, is easy solution. Come lay with me, my sweet. I have missed you," I cajoled, rubbing my cock as I spoke. His prick did not go down. It grew fatter. I licked my lips. "There are ways to do sexing up for no hips. Sit on my face."

"*Stan…*"

"No? Okay, we will sixty-nine with you on top. I am good at sucking dick." I waggled an eyebrow while freeing my cock from my baggy shorts, the worn elastic band settling under my balls. My husband frowned but his dick grew even thicker. "Okay then, no number sex. Hand sex with much kissing. Gentle. Maybe a finger in a good place." His tangled eyebrows eased. "Two fingers at most."

"You could talk the Devil into buying a hibachi," he sighed, his gaze sliding down over me.

"Yes, I am good with making sweet words of love. Now come here so I can enjoy your body. It has been too long."

He moved gingerly, peeling off his shorts then locking the bedroom door. The sniffles of a few dogs poking their noses under the crack could be heard as Erik eased himself back into bed, his pupils fat, his lips wet. I linked a hand behind his head, dove my fingers into those soft curls, and led his mouth to mine. He was timid at first, shuffling closer with great care, his tongue meeting mine as if this were our first kiss. That nervousness faded as the kiss deepened. He held himself above me, careful of my incisions, but soon enough I had him breathless and leaking. My fingers closed around his shaft, inching him closer, higher, until he gave in and slung a muscular leg over my face. His cock bobbed in front of me, tickling my nose as he held himself up, arms locked, lips skimming my cockhead.

"Don't let me hurt you," he whispered before falling on my prick like a man starved.

I gasped at the warm wet pleasure for Erik had a skilled tongue and knew what I liked. As he sucked with vigor, I wet my middle finger then moved my head just an inch. The soft end of his cock brushed my lips, temping me, teasing me, so I flicked the slit to gather the pre-cum there. He shuddered and groaned around my cock. I felt my balls draw up. Someday soon I would love him long and hard as we both liked but for now, it seemed, this would be a quickie. That, I could live with.

I slid my finger around the edge of his hole, eyes closed, inhaling the musky aroma of my husband, then began sucking on his fat cockhead. He moaned low and long. I eased my slick finger into him and got a whimper of pleasure I knew well. He pushed back on my finger, eager for more, his mouth working me expertly. A white-hot burst went off at the base of my spine as I hooked my finger. Erik gasped around me, sucking in cool air, and my orgasm rolled over me like a tidal wave. It was hard to come and not buck up or roll my hips to get deeper but his weight on my belly kept me flat. I found his prostate, scraped it, and then sighed as he jerked and spent down my throat. I threw my free arm over his back to keep him in place so I could get every delicious drop.

"Stan... oh hell. That was... wow," he whispered, his lips resting on my still swollen cock, his prick pulsing on my tongue. Soon the tremors eased and with infinite care he eased off me, turning gingerly on the bed then, because he knew I loved it, bending over to kiss me hard. His tongue and mine mixing and sharing our essences. When he sat back his cheeks were flushed under his new gold whiskers. He was an angel come down from the heavens and he was *all* mine.

"Yes, I agree. Lots of wow." I smiled while my overheated body cooled. A robin trilled outside, greeting another new day. "I am feeling much better today."

"So I see." He eased himself down, bracketing his hands on either side of my head to drop a kiss to the tip of my nose. "I'm glad your pain is easing but don't get crazy and overdo."

I frowned as he pulled on his shorts then began aiding me to leave my bed. This was a tricky thing but with Erik home the shuffling about was helped tremendously as he could take more of my weight than anyone else in our home. Soon, with some mild cursing from me, both my feet were on the floor. I crutched my way into the bathroom, Erik chattering away as we both showered, his body pressed to mine made me half-hard but there was no encore. Erik eyed my pert prick with a naughty smile but washed my back instead of my erection, falling into nurse mode. Sadly times.

It took us longer to get downstairs but when we arrived Mama was already awake, coffee brewing, and a large breakfast on the horizon. The children soon arrived, after I'd gotten comfortable in a chair, both girls sleepy but talkative.

"Where is your brother?" I asked while platters of over easy eggs, sausage, fruit, yogurt, and strong coffee for the adults were served.

Margo sipped orange juice, but Eva poured herself a large mug of coffee, something I still was not used to seeing. How had this child grown up so fast? I was truly getting older, the silver at my temples and throughout the hair in my chinny-chin-chin attested to this.

"He's sleeping in," Margo announced.

Erik scowled at his plate of food as Mama took her seat and reached for our hands. Nothing was said as Mama offered up a blessing in Russian but as soon as the amens rang out Erik spoke up.

"He knows we have animals to take to the vet this morning," Erik said, glancing from Margo to Eva.

Both girls shrugged.

"We can get them, Papa," Eva chimed up, always ready to defend her younger siblings. "It's just Bruno, Louisa, and Maribel. Margo can take Maribel in the cat carrier, and you and I can have Bruno and Louisa on leashes."

Both dogs who were getting shots lifted their heads from the floor at the mention of their names then sighed as if they knew they were going to get poked in the backside soon. Maribel, Margo's shy calico cat, was probably in Margo's room under the bed, meaning Erik would have to fish the cat out then place her into the carrier. Much hissing and clawing would take place, leaving Erik needing band-aids and kisses from his loving spouse.

"Let Noah rest. Boys his age are always sleeping or eating," Mama said while spooning another egg onto Erik's plate. "Eat. You are too pale and skinny. Like a kikimora."

Erik gave me a look. I rolled a shoulder then dove into my food. My day would consist of doing exercises at home, reading a good book about gay ghost hunters from the old days, and enjoying a walk around the block with Mama. She and I moved at the same speed now.

The morning sped by after the mass exodus of dogs and cranky cat to the vet. Erik went to the barn for morning skate, which would be nothing more than suiting up and team morale-building. They needed it, because Toronto was hot, and my poor Erik was aching. I helped Mama clean the kitchen, then took myself outside to read in the sunshine. It felt good to be able to sit and read. I'd missed it a great deal. King stretched out beside me on the back porch, his heavy brown tail thumping on the boards. I reached down to stroke his soft fur, the sun making the gray on his muzzle shine.

"We are both old men, my friend," I whispered to the dog then read for a bit. When I woke up from reading, I rose, King on my heels, to find Mama in the living room working on some needlepoint while watching Kelly and Mark. Mama *loved* Kelly and Mark. "Have we heard from Noah yet?" I asked and she shook her head. "Okay, I will go give him a shake."

"I will do it," she said, laying her needlepoint aside.

"No, I will go. Sit, rest, you work too hard."

"You are a godsend," she said then smiled at me as a mother who adores her son does. "Your sister is coming over later with the little ones."

"Ah, good. Tell her to bring some of her apple cake for her poor ailing brother," I called as I began climbing the stairs. It was tricky but I was improving. A little bit each day.

My son did not respond when I tapped his door with a crutch. Nor did he stir when I rapped harder. I opened the door a crack, always aware that young adults did not like parents dashing in to their space. Not that I dashed anywhere at the moment…

"Noah, is time to get up. Is nearly noon and we have the game this evening, much excitement, in the box," I called, easing the door open wider when no sound but his soft snores bounced back to me.

His curtains were drawn but the sun sliced through a gap in the navy blue draperies, the strip falling on Noah's form huddled under a duvet, nothing but the top of his blond head showing. I pushed the door wider then frowned at the state of his bedroom. Again, we did not push our way into our children's rooms because they were entitled to privacy. I recalled quite well what it was like to be a young person with raging hormones. I also recalled how little I cared as a teenager about the state of my room but this…

Well, this room was more than untidy, it was slovenly. Clothes lay everywhere, dirty bowls were piled on the dresser and his computer desk, and water bottles covered the floor. Dozens and dozens of bottles, possibly enough to stock the Railers bench for a few games. We would need to make more than a monthly spot-check on the kids if this was how the boy wished to live. The area stank of unwashed boy and hockey equipment. His gear lay tossed in the corner under a poster of Goku, a character from *Dragon Ball* series of anime and cartoons, that Noah thought was cool. Or rad. Or whatever term the kids were using nowadays. Empty potato chip and cheese puffs bags were everywhere, as were takeout dishes, brown McDonald's bags, and candy wrappers.

"So old," I whispered to myself as I made my way through the refuse piles to the young man sleeping so soundly in his wide bed. "Noah, it is time to get up."

I sat down beside him, grunting a little as I did, then reached out to give him a shake. He mumbled something, shifted to his stomach, and fell right back to sleep. We did this a few more times then I began to grow concerned. I knew that young minds and bodies needed more rest than us old folks, but he seemed almost unable to wake. I placed a hand on his brow. He didn't seem feverish, but his face was thin, his cheekbones pronounced. He'd gotten leaner of late, but we had attributed it to a growth spurt and the fact he was now skating every single day, sometimes for several hours. We would need to see that he ate more and better. This shrine to junk food was bad. A growing athlete needed healthy food.

He growled and lashed out, his words hard to decipher.

"Noah, are you not feeling well?" I asked, using the back of my fingers to lift a sticky strand of hair from his cheek.

"Just sleepy," he mumbled, his lashes fluttering. "Gotta pee."

He threw off the covers, stumbled to his bathroom, and slammed the door in my face. Ah teenagers. Such rays of sunshine and joy. He emerged a few minutes later, his dusky blue Railers shorts hanging off his hips. I studied him intently. His body seemed much leaner than I had realized, his stomach concave, his skin sallow, and his eyes dull.

"Noah, are you sick? Should I call the good doctor?" I asked.

"Go away." He wiggled back under the covers, pulled them over his head, and then fell right back asleep. A weight began to settle on my shoulders. Something was off with our youngest child. Looking around the room at the darkness I began to fear that perhaps he was depressed.

"Okay, Son, rest a bit longer. But you will have to be up at noon," I whispered, placing my hand on his hip. He jerked away from my touch, snarling like a rabid raccoon, and told me to leave him the fuck alone. That was not our sunshiny boy at all. Easing myself up I headed downstairs to greet Erik, my shoulders tight with worry.

My husband and I were going to have a long talk about our baby boy.

Chapter Six

The lights of the arena buzzed overhead, and the sea of Railers blue was everything we needed tonight. It was game four, and we were 3–0 down in this round, and Toronto fans in the crowd, pockets of white, were loud with excitement because the Railers were on the verge of losing this and stopping one round short of fighting for the Stanley Cup. We were so close, but it had been torture getting there.

"Fuck," Adler muttered under his breath.

I wasn't sure he meant for anyone else to hear. I'd seen him pacing in the weight room, his husband Layton Fox, our newly minted executive head of social media, talking to him, and trying to catch his arm every time he passed. We all put on brave, confident faces, but when it came down to it, the mood in the locker room was serious. And cold. And lonely without Stan.

I wasn't someone who believed in miracles, but shit, we needed one tonight. The odds were stacked against us, and even though I felt the weight of collective hope from my teammates, the coaching staff, and every fan in the stands, my heart refused to stop hurting. I couldn't see Stan in the VIP box, but I knew he was up there, because he and the girls had met me in staff parking to wish us luck and was probably more nervous than I was. The fact he couldn't be on the ice, defending our goal, was a wound that would never heal, the team's normal last line of defense, my personal hero, and I couldn't even imagine the frustration bubbling up inside him. Eva and Margo were there as well, both so excited and I wanted to win for them, to show them that no matter how bleak the odds, their dad could rise to the challenge.

I just wasn't sure it would happen.

"Okay?" Adler tapped my shin gently.

I met his gaze. "Yeah," I said, bullish, confident, not at all pissed that our year was likely to end tonight. I didn't know why I couldn't shove the thoughts of losing aside—that was what hockey players did. They shoved negativity aside, they relied on luck and hope, and forced positivity.

"How's Noah?"

And there it was. The missing person from the box, one I'd come to associate with luck, joy, and hope: Noah. He had the flu, or so Stan told me. At least I think that was what he was trying to tell me, just that Noah was home ill, and sent his love. I hadn't expected him not to be here, and the thought of my lucky charm not being close was hard. Every win, every goal, every celebration had him and the girls at its heart. It felt wrong not having him there, like going into battle without a trusted weapon.

"Flu," I said.

"Poor kid."

The line shuffled forward a little, Ten, coming up six years our captain, tense and waiting to lead the team out on the ice.

"Two minutes," someone called from the side, counting down with us to hitting the ice.

Maybe I *have the flu as well?* Maybe that was why I felt so tight with stress and couldn't find the sweet spot where the real world slipped away and I was just Erik, skater, hockey player, goal scorer, winner. I'd never been a superstitious man, not really. Sure, I had my game day rituals like every other hockey player. The exact order of putting on my gear, the way I taped my stick, the last-minute visualization before stepping onto the ice. But today, those rituals seem shallow, dwarfed by the weight of emotions threatening to overtake me.

Next to me Adler went quiet, and that wasn't right either—he was energy and spark and teasing but he was silent. I tapped his shin in return, and we exchanged smiles.

Forced smiles.

On the bench, every word of the national anthem was a reminder tonight was not just about hockey; it was about family, love, hope, and belief. I couldn't control the outcome of the game, but I could control the effort I put in, and I vowed to give it everything I had. For the Railers. For Stan, Eva, Margo. And for Noah.

For me.

I just wish Noah was here.

Ten was up against the Toronto captain in the face-off. He won the puck and hope flooded me. Coming back to win four games in a row had been done before, and maybe that would be us. The chilled air of the rink nipped at my face, but the sting was nothing compared to the pressure of hope I felt in my chest. We could do this. The clock seemed to change both agonizingly slow and terrifyingly fast as we fought tooth and nail, every move calculated, each pass and shot full of desperate optimism. Only the resounding clang of the puck hitting the pipes became an all-too-familiar soundtrack of the evening. Once, twice, three times... more... every time it sounded, it felt like a punch to the gut, a cruel tease of what could have been. The tension in the arena was intense. Fans on the edge of their seats, screams of support every time we got a look on goal, and we were in the third and final period, the score at two fat goose eggs, tied with nothing, and the hope bloomed.

Bryan was tall and impenetrable in our goal, and he was having the game of his life. Every save he made sent waves of relief through me. He was a wall, a fortress, our last hope against Toronto, the same as Stan would have been. But with just five minutes left, the unthinkable happened. A quick pass, a shot that tumbled over and over, deflecting off a skate, and the red light behind our net was glaring. The deafening cheer from the Toronto fans was a cruel jolt back to reality. I glanced over at Bryan, his posture deflated, his eyes reflecting the heartbreak we all felt.

One–nothing to Toronto.

Five minutes to go.

Those last five minutes felt like an eternity. We

threw everything we had at them, every last ounce of energy, skill, and determination. But the universe, it seemed, had other plans. The final buzzer sounded, sealing our fate, and we were out of the Stanley Cup. The weight of the loss bore down on us all, but every one of us skated over to Bryan, placing a hand on his shoulder, trying to offer some semblance of comfort. Words failed me; in times like these, they often did.

Adler and Ten skated back to the center of the ice, starting the line to congratulate Toronto. Chins tipped, they were stoic, and as we moved along the line offering our praise to the opposing team for a job well done, the exhaustion and disappointment were obvious. Then, the silence in our locker room was suffocating, each of us processing the loss in our own way. The journey to the Stanley Cup had been intense, emotional, and tonight, utterly heart-wrenching. We had come so close, only to have our dreams crushed at the very end, and every one of us felt it.

"We fought hard," Ten said, when no one else wanted to say a thing. "We tried everything."

There was a murmur of agreement, and then more silence.

Adler cursed. "It's fucking shit, that's what it is."

This time it was as if everyone sighed at the same

time, then someone else cursed, then another. As I unlaced my skates, I added my own curse, and then I knew...

I just wanted to go home.

Exiting the stadium was a blur of condolences, pats on the back, and whispered regrets. Ten and I hovered around Bryan, but his partner was waiting outside, and it would be on Gatlin to support Bryan when we were all home.

"You took us this far," Ten reassured Bryan, squeezing his shoulder, and then he glanced at Gatlin, who nodded. Bryan was in good hands.

As I approached the parking lot, the sight of our SUV brought an unexpected lump to my throat. Stan was in the passenger seat, his crutches resting on the door, Eva and Margo stood beside the vehicle, waiting for me. I hadn't taken more than a few steps before they bolted towards me, wrapping their arms around my waist, and loving me hard; they didn't care about the loss; they cared about me.

"It's okay, Dad," Eva said first. "It's okay."

"It's okay now I'm getting hugged," I said, as Margo burrowed into my arms.

Aching and tired I pulled away as they climbed into the car, only to lock eyes with Stan. He knew the weight of my disappointment, just as I recognized the frustration in his eyes—the sting of being sidelined during our most critical game.

"Too strong from Toronto," Stan began, standing, supported by crutches, his voice carrying a tinge of sadness, but then he half smiled. "My hero," he added, as I limped toward him, and half fell into his strong hold.

I wasn't anyone's hero tonight, I hadn't pulled out a magic hat trick, I hadn't scored a game-winning goal, and from the way I ached, all I'd *actually* managed was survive another game.

"Is Bryan okay?" he asked after a while, as I leaned there and inhaled the scent of him, genuine concern evident in his tone.

"I think he's taking it hard," I admitted, thinking of our young goalie's dejected posture after that lone goal.

Stan nodded. "I've sent text for him to bounce back." Then he smiled at me. "Let's go home," he said as I climbed into the driver's seat. God I hurt, and I wished I'd thought to order a car service, given Stan couldn't drive.

"Eva, can you drive for me?" I asked when just pressing the gas pedal hurt.

"Sure, Dad," she said, and we swapped places.

In the back Margo leaned into me, and even

buckled in, she was just what I needed, and I think I might have even dozed off.

"What!" Stan exclaimed and startled me back to the here and now.

"What?" I asked because Stan sounded panicked.

My heart skipped a beat as we headed up the driveway. The flashing lights of an ambulance illuminated our home in an eerie glow. Panic surged through me.

"Oh god, Mama?" Stan whispered, his voice shaky.

Eva pulled the car to one side of the ambulance, the four of us spilling out of the car, Stan crutching toward the paramedics, me closing in as fast as I could.

But it wasn't Mama who needed help—it was Noah. Terror clenched my heart as I saw the paramedics surrounding him, their movements swift and purposeful. My mind raced, trying to grasp the situation, to understand what was happening.

"I tried. He just fell down. He fell down!" Stan's mama wailed, falling against her son. "He fell down. I tried. I tried!" She was hysterical, I was numb, the girls crying, and Stan was at my side, his hand gripping mine, silent support in the chaos.

Paramedic one talked over the noise, paramedic two silent and checking for signs of…

Life?

My world crumbled. No.

Noah!

They rolled him onto a gurney, and in the flashing light he was deathly pale and still.

"We're taking him to St. Margarets," paramedic one announced as they lifted the gurney into the ambulance.

"I'll drive," Eva announced as we went back to the SUV, Mama staying at the front door, crying, and wringing her hands. I hadn't even spared a thought about the house, the unlocked front door, or our security gates being wide open.

I couldn't think at all.

We followed the ambulance in silence, abandoning the SUV in the closest parking lot to the Emergency room entrance, then hurrying in to be guided to a room to one side.

"It was flu," I said to the door. "Just flu. What happened? Stan?"

Stan was white, stiff, staring at the same door as if he were willing it to open. He didn't say anything.

"Fuck! Stan!" I half-shouted at him, my voice loud in the small room.

Margo started and grabbed on to Eva who patted her and winced. I went for the door, yanking it open, and finding a medic on the other side.

"Mr...."

"Gunnarson, Noah's dad, Gunnarson-Lyamin, we're Noah's dads." The words tripped over each other.

The medic slipped into the room, closed the door behind them, and I read his name. Dr. Garcia. His badge was a teddy bear, with the name on its belly. The fuck? Where was Noah?

"I'm Doctor Luca Garcia, and I'm the resident pediatrician. Would you like to sit down?"

"No, I don't want to sit down!" I almost yelled.

Then I felt Stan's hand on my arm, comforting me or holding me back, I didn't know. I wanted to shrug him off. He was supposed to be watching Noah, he was the one at home. He told me Noah had the flu!

My thoughts spiraled into fear, and then regret and shame. I didn't shrug Stan off, because this wasn't on him. I didn't know what was wrong with Noah, but this was no one's fault. Right?

"Thank you for your patience," Dr. Garcia began. "Noah is going to be okay," he began, and my chest tightened. "But let me explain Noah's situation."

I tightened my grip on Stan's hand, bracing myself for what was to come.

"Noah has collapsed due to complications associated with diabetes." He paused a moment, probably searching our expressions for what we knew of diabetes.

"Specifically, it seems he experienced diabetic ketoacidosis, or DKA." Dr. Garcia's voice was steady and soothing, but my head was spinning. "I won't sugarcoat this. Diabetes is a severe condition that occurs when the body doesn't produce enough insulin. Without insulin, the body starts to break down fat as fuel, producing ketones, which can build up in the blood and become acidic."

My heart pounded in my ears. "He had flu," I murmured. "Just the flu."

Dr. Garcia nodded, but then he continued. "The immediate *concern* with DKA is the high level of acid in the blood, which can affect vital organs if not treated promptly." He paused again, giving us a moment to process the information and Stan gripped my arm tighter. "But we've started Noah on insulin therapy to help bring his blood sugar levels back to normal. Along with fluids and electrolytes to prevent dehydration and address the acid-base imbalance."

I wanted to be level-headed and understand what

the doctor was saying, but I would make a deal with the devil right now to make sure Noah was safe. "What now?" I blurted.

Dr. Garcia sighed. "Noah has type 1 diabetes, which is a lifelong condition. But with proper management—regular blood sugar monitoring, insulin therapy, and dietary adjustments—he can lead a full and active life."

"Will he die?" Margo asked softly.

I swallowed hard, images of athletic, vibrant Noah flashing before my eyes. "No," I said, and pulled her and Eva into my side as best I could. Fear, confusion, and guilt flooded me but was mixed with a fierce determination. Noah was strong. We would help him.

We *weren't* losing Noah.

Dr. Garcia offered a comforting smile. "What your dad said," he offered. "Would you like to see him? He's sleeping." He shot me a glance that implied it wasn't so much sleeping as unconsciousness, but to get to go in the room with him was everything.

"Let's go."

Chapter Seven

STAN

I am now convinced there is no hell on earth worse than sitting beside your child as they lie in a hospital bed.

If I never have to experience this nightmare again, I will go to meet my maker a happy man. Children should not get sick, not sick like this, not so sick they have tubes and machines attached to them. No. This is wrong. This is not at all in God's plan for little ones. I refused to believe the Almighty would allow such a thing to happen to a boy as good and bright as Noah. I reached out to touch his arm, careful of the needles bruising his skin, as our boy rested peacefully. Erik sat across the room from me, dark circles under his eyes, silent and still. Too still. I knew he did not pray as I had been doing for hours now. His thoughts were elsewhere, somewhere dark and trying, I suspected, given how tight his jaw was.

I would have liked to press him about where his mind was, what he was thinking, but right now all I could do was focus on Noah as I petitioned God to forgive me for being such a bad father.

The door opened, a slim nurse entering, her dark gaze moving from my husband to me. "We'll be serving breakfast soon. Would you like trays brought up?"

"No, I am not thinking of food right now," I replied, my voice scratchy from not using it for hours. "But please bring some for my husband."

"I'm good," Erik announced, his tone dour as he rose with a groan that made the nurse glance at him with concern. "I need coffee." He shifted to the bed, brushed a kiss to Noah's brow, and then struggled around the nurse standing awkwardly just inside the doorway, her hands folded in front of her as she studied the stethoscope resting on her pink scrub top covered with dancing lemurs. Scrubs, yes? That was what the nurses wore to work? Ugh, my brain was failing as lack of sleep and stress began to set in.

"Would you please grab—" I managed to get out before he gave me a look that could burn through a brick building. I withered under his glare. He too knew this was on me. I should have seen our son's condition worsening. I'd been home for weeks now. Weeks. Doing nothing but working on my rehab, my only concern returning to the ice. To the game. To the cheers of the crowd. What a pitiful, self-centered slug I was.

Erik left, the nurse exited, and I wiggled around in my chair, my ass and hips aching from sitting for so long. But they would have to use a crowbar to get me from this seat. Here I would sit, my new hips petrifying from lack of use, until my boy smiled at me.

I rubbed at my eyes, dry now, all the tears being shed overnight. My phone lay on the rolling table beside a pitcher of water and a box of tissues, turned off hours ago after I had texted Mama to let her know what was taking place inside Noah's young body. Diabetes. I *knew* I should not have let Mama buy all those cookies the children coveted so much. I should not have let Erik treat them to ice cream after a good game. I should not have taken them trick-or-treating all those years. My God above, how had I allowed this to happen to my little boy?!

Someone knocked on the door, a gentle rap, subtle. A doctor perhaps, or the nurse coming with coffee or a Danish. My stomach rumbled but I ignored it. What right did I have to treat myself to sweets when my boy lay sick and weak? None. I had no right.

"Come," I called, watching Noah in the hopes that my voice would rouse him, but he slept on, his eyelashes gold and thick as they rested on his sallow cheeks. "You can take back any food for I am not hungry."

"Oh crap, well, I guess I'll have to eat this Whopper all by myself," Tennant whispered as he crept into the room. I shifted around on the chair, wincing at the pull at my surgery sites, to see my best friend pause at the end of the bed. "You know that they say Elvis loved Burger King."

"Yes, I know this. He was the king and so he would love king food. I am not hungry; you may eat it." I slid forward to take some of the pressure off my tailbone.

"Seriously, you have to eat it. I forced some poor kid at the drive-through window to cook me this and add fries when they were only doing breakfast food." Ten went closer, waving the bag back and forth as if tempting a dog with a bone. My belly snarled at the smell of flame-broiled goodness and French fries. I shook my head. Ten frowned, walked to me, and shoved the bag into my chest. I mumbled about pushy friends in Russian. "Whatever you just said I am sure it was thanks buddy." Ten then bent down to press a kiss to my unwashed hair then hug me to him. I linked an arm around his middle, allowing my nose to press into his Railers hoodie and drew in a few dozen shaky breaths. "He's going to be okay." I drew back, opened the bag, and pulled out the somewhat flattened burger. "Eat that. You need to keep your strength up, my man." I scowled at the food then sighed. Yes, he was right. "I saw Erik outside on the phone, talking to the girls at home and your mother. He said you needed food. I made him take a burger too. He called me a pushy asshole but went over to sit by the window to eat. So yeah, eat."

"You are most pushy friend," I stated before peeling back the wrapper to take a bite. Mm, yes, this was delicious. No wonder the King enjoyed it so much. "Thank you for being pushy friend."

"Someone has to do it," he teased, going around the bed to peel open a drapery panel to let some sun shine into the brightly painted room. There were little ducks and smiling chicks on the pale yellow walls, all fat and happy. They should stick fat ducklings on all hospital room walls instead of sterile white like I had stared at for days after my surgery. "Soren is taking a stuffed coyote to school to get the team to sign it, for their biggest fan and all that.'

"Good, yes, Noah will like this." I swiped at the ketchup on my chin with a crinkled paper napkin, half the massive burger gone already. "He is sickly."

"Yeah, I know. Jared and I have been peppering Erik with questions all night. Dude, you really should have your phone on," he said, resting his backside on the air-conditioning unit under the window overlooking the Susquehanna River.

"No, I am not making phone calls to people. I need my head here on Noah," I replied around a mouthful of ground beef, bun, and all the trimmings including extra pickles. Tennant was a very good friend for only the best of friends knew you liked extra pickles. "Erik is handling all that."

"Is that really fair to place all of that on him though?" Ten asked, his gaze steady. I swallowed and averted my gaze. "I'm not trying to ride you at a time like this because I know that if it was one of my kids in that bed, I would be utter batshit crazy, but he's just as freaked out as you are. Maybe just think about it?"

"You are marriage counselor now?" I asked, the prick of his words wounding me, for I knew they were true.

"Nope, not even close. Just a dumb puck-pusher.

What I am though is married, and while I love this kid as if he was one of my own," he waved a hand at Noah sound asleep in that big white bed, "I'm seeing things from the outside. And Erik is about to crack. So, stop hiding in here and being that big mean Russian bear you like other players to think you are, and just be the Stan that we all know and love."

"Hmm, you are sounding like counselor to me." Tennant shrugged and smiled just a bit. If I could reach him, I would hug him once more for he was the truest sort of friend. He would tell you the truth if you were being an ass. That was a rare thing. "I will turn on phone as soon as I am done eating."

"Cool, so Jared and the kids and all the guys are sending love and hugs so make sure you drop into the team chat."

"Da, yes, of course." I shoved some fries into my mouth, and we fell into a warm silence, one that bolstered me with its quiet support. After I was done and had washed down the meal with some tepid water from a plastic pitcher, I pushed to my feet. "He will be okay," I told Tennant.

"Of course, he will be."

"I am not sure I am such a good parent right now," I confessed just as Erik entered with coffee.

Tennant stared at me as if I was mad, but I ignored him and lumbered into the bathroom to pee. I'd not done so all night, so the relief was great.

I lingered afterwards, washing my hands and face, running my wet fingers through my lank hair. I stared at myself, my weight on my crutches, and stared at the lines around my eyes. Life lines Mama called them, laugh lines Erik liked to say when he kissed them, wrinkles my children called them. I'd done so much in my life, won Stanley Cups, played in the Olympics, and had heard my name mentioned for a future slot in the Hockey Hall of Fame. So many achievements, so many days and weeks and months and years devoted to hockey. A lifetime of dedication and sacrifice to the sport but what had it gotten me? A child so sick he'd passed out with only his aged grandmother there to tend to him. I should have been home, not at the game enjoying myself, talking to the press about when I would return. I should have been home last night. Perhaps I should have been home for the entire season. Perhaps for all the seasons that we had children in our lives.

"Stan." Erik opened the door a crack, enough to push his head through to find me examining myself in the mirror. "I have coffee."

"Is he awake?"

"Not yet. Come out please." I crutched my sorry ass back into the room, noting that Tennant was no longer here. I glanced at Erik who had taken over my seat by the bed, leaving me the chair by the window. "Ten left fifteen minutes ago."

Oh. Had I been in that tiny bath with the open shower and emergency pull cord for over a quarter of an hour? How was that possible?

"I would have liked to say goodbye to him," I stated, easing myself down with a moan then reaching for the large cup of coffee on the windowsill.

"Then you should have come out of the bathroom," Erik said flatly, his focus on Noah as he sipped his coffee.

"Yes, that is true. I lost time…" I didn't know how to explain what I had been doing staring at myself in a looking glass for so long.

Erik stared at me over his cup, his usually bright blue eyes listless. "You need to contact your mother. She's beside herself, speaking to me in Russian which I'm not really able to follow when she starts racing along."

"Yes, of course, I will call Mama." I nodded as Erik flipped my phone to me, the Android sailing over Noah's legs to land in my hand. An easy save. If only my lower half were as good as my upper half I'd be playing now instead of—

"And the girls. They want to hear from you. Eva is holding things down, but she's just as scared as the rest of us even if she won't show it. She keeps everything inside. You need to let her know that we've got things under control at this end so she can get some rest."

"Yes, yes, I am going to do so. I know where my faults are, trust me. I do not need you telling me what a terrible father I am!"

His eyes flared. I blinked at the ferocity of my words.

"Papa," Noah called. The lone word scratchy and weak but the most joyous sound I had ever heard. Not even the choirs of the angels could have sounded any sweeter. Erik flew to his feet, nearly dumping his coffee into his lap as I struggled to get up with one arm. "I feel terrible…"

"We know," Erik whispered, sitting beside our son, his eyes wet with unshed tears as he cradled one of Noah's small hands. I moved closer, one crutch under each arm, to gaze down at the tiny boy who owned such a large portion of my heart. "You'll be better soon. We're all going to do better." Erik threw me a pointed look that sliced into me like a knife.

"Yes, we will do better," I croaked, my eyes also growing dewy now. Amazing, as I had been sure there were no tears left to cry after the awful night that had just passed. "The doctors say you will be just fine, little bunny."

"What happened?" Noah asked, his gaze flicking from Erik to me to the room, fear now replacing confusion. "Am I super sick? Am I going to die?"

"Absolutely not," Erik rushed to say as he gave Noah's hand a squeeze. I shook my head so hard that I made myself woozy. "You're going to be fine. You have diabetes." Noah's blue eyes rounded. "That is something that is easily handled, Noah. With medication, exercise, and a healthy diet you'll live a long, productive life."

Noah glanced from Erik to me. "Will I be able to play hockey?"

"Yes, of course, you will be able to do whatever it is you wish for many hundreds of years." I nodded then caught onto what I had said. "Okay, so maybe not hundreds of years, but for many long years. You do not have to fear for your future, my sweet one."

"Okay, if you say so." He asked for a drink of water, which we gave him, then we rang for the nurse.

She arrived with smiles and cheer, chattering as she took his vitals. Erik and I stood in opposite corners, his attention on our child, mine on the cold tiles under my feet. I wished they would crack open and swallow me up whole.

Chapter Eight

We sat with Noah for a while longer, but he was tired, it was late, almost ten without us even realizing, and somehow we'd passed an entire day of Noah being here, of Noah being diabetic, of the entirety of his world shifting.

Margo and Eva had left, taking the car back home, but it would take bigger men than us to take us from Noah's side. I didn't know what to say to Stan, not when he was fighting his own demons as much as I was.

I should have been there.

I should have noticed.

And the sneaky whisper that slipped into my rational thinking, why hadn't Stan noticed?

With Noah sleeping, Stan excused himself to

find coffee, and this time I wasn't letting the whispers win. I found him down by the coffee machine, watching as he waited in the dim light of the hospital corridor, his hands white-knuckled on his crutches, his brow furrowed with the weight of self-reproach.

"Stan," I interrupted his erratic orbit.

He stopped and stared at me; his gray eyes shadowed with pain. "I'm sorry," he blurted, his eyes brightening with emotion. "He had some flu, I thinked, I was... just flu..." he added as if he was trying to convince himself that maybe the doctors were wrong.

I reached out, placing my hands on his shoulders, grounding him, shoving blame aside, and what-ifs, and trusting he'd understand how much I loved him. Stan could spiral, I'd seen it before, and given I wanted his love and support and one of his big smiles right now, I was guessing he needed the same thing from me.

"Listen to me," I urged, locking my gaze with his. "You couldn't have known Noah was sick. None of us did."

He shook his head, his voice barely a whisper, "But I'm not seeing dad things." He added a sentence in Russian, and I didn't know the words, but I felt the meaning in my soul. "I'm dad," he repeated, and his voice cracked.

"And you're a great dad," I assured him with as much conviction as I could muster while my own heart hurt. "We both are, and we've done nothing but love and care for Noah. This illness crept up on all of us. And right now, Noah doesn't need either of us drowning in guilt. He needs us to be a team, as we've always been."

The flickering fluorescent light overhead cast a sterile glow on his face, and he closed his eyes, before tugging me in with one arm. Fuck. I wanted to cry, I wanted to shout and wail at whoever put our beautiful son in the hospital. Where was the fairness in this? He was a good kid.

But he's alive.

He will live.

It might be hard, but the doctor assured us he'd do okay.

I had to believe him.

Stan held me so tight I couldn't move, and I buried my face in his neck.

"I'm sorry," he said again. "I'm sorry."

"I'm sorry, too," I added. "Did we do something wrong? Did we… did I… what if his birth mom was here? Would she have seen it?" Fuck, I was losing my shit now. Freja wasn't Noah's mom other than biologically, was happy and focused on her career as a journalist traveling the world, and hell, I didn't even know where she was right now.

"No," Stan interrupted and pushed me away a little so he could tip my chin. "We are the best for little rabbit."

"I'm so scared."

"Scared too," Stan offered, and then it was my turn to pull him close, wrapping my arms around him in a firm embrace, sharing the strength between us that had always seemed to be enough to face the world.

"Noah's going to look to us for how to handle this," I whispered into his ear. "We've got to show him that we can handle it and stow all this guilt shit."

Stan gave a silent nod against my shoulder, and I guess that was the beginning of the end for self-imposed blame, and probably mine too.

No one could have seen this happen.

"We'll get through this," I breathed, believing it for his sake, for Noah's, and maybe a little for my own. "We'll learn everything we need to, we'll make adjustments, and we'll still be the family that we've always been. Nothing changes that. Not diabetes, not anything."

Pulling back just enough to see his face, I searched his eyes and saw the flicker of resolve reigniting there.

"Together," he said, then smiled. "Like Elvis and Blue Suede Shoes."

"Yeah." I returned his smile. "Yeah."

It was a day later when Oliver "Cowboy" Cowan defenseman with New York, showed up without warning at the hospital.

Courtesy of Ten, apparently.

"Hi, guys." He waved. "Ten said you needed me," he added, standing in the doorway as the three of us glanced up, startled.

Stan growled. Oliver was one of those D-men who hovered around the net, and I knew Stan had big feelings about players like him. Annoying. Assholes. Or as he called them—buzzy bees.

Noah was the one who actually strung words together.

"You're Oliver Cowan," he said with respect.

"Sure am, kid," Oliver responded, stepping just inside the room, and extending a hand to me, which I shook, and then to Stan, who refused to uncross his arms, and just stared.

Yep. He wasn't fond of Oliver Cowan.

"Okay if I come in?" he asked.

I was confused. "Ten sent you?"

Now it was Oliver's turn to be confused. "He didn't tell you?"

Stan muttered something in Russian, and I sent him a quelling glance, because it was clear there was a reason for Ten to… wait…

"You have diabetes," I exclaimed.

Oliver twisted his mouth into a parody of a smile. "But more importantly, I have great two-way defense skills with the twenty-third highest point tally of all defensemen of all time," he corrected.

"Buzz, buzz," Stan muttered.

Oliver reached out to shake a hand again, and this time Stan took it, and the two big men faced off against each other like warriors on a battlefield. I stepped between them before Stan made some comment about… well, about anything… and guided the conversation back to Noah.

"Noah has just been diagnosed," I said, and couldn't fail to see the flare of something in Oliver's eyes. It wasn't pity, or anything like that, it was understanding and compassion.

"Yep, that's why Ten sent me. He saw how I handled things firsthand when I was at the Olympics and thought I could help a bit. Can I?" He waved at Noah, and I stepped back and let him pass.

What was he going to do? Would he say something that would upset Noah? Ten had sent him. Ten must've thought he's okay. I exchanged quick glances with Stan, who nodded.

"Sure," I said, and took a seat the other side of the bed.

Oliver folded his big frame into the tiny hospital chair next to Noah, which wasn't built for hockey player asses, and then held out a fist to bump, which Noah bumped back. He'd seen a lot of big-name players, but I'd never seen him this tongue-tied. I checked the machine monitoring his vitals and was relieved his sugar levels seemed to be in the okay region. They would be in here, given everything was so balanced, and he was cared for.

But what would happen when he came home? What if we dropped the baton again, and fucked up?

"So hey, Noah," he began. "I hear you're joining the one club nobody really signs up for," he began as he wriggled in the chair.

"Yeah." Noah nodded; his expression uncertain but with a hint of curiosity. Oliver "Cowboy" Cowan was a solid third line defenseman with New York, and had been since he was drafted, not only that but he was just about to move into his fifteenth year of playing professional hockey, which had to count for something. I just hoped to hell this was the right thing to do. A small, scared part of me wanted Oliver to explain how diabetes was this impossible thing, so I could keep Noah safe, but it was the treacherous part. The rest of me wanted Noah to do everything any kid wanted to do, without limits or restrictions.

"So, diabetes eh?" Oliver began. "I know it's probably a little scary right now, thinking about how this is gonna change things for you. But let me tell you something, buddy—it doesn't have to stop you from doing anything you love." His voice still held that Texas twang from the town he'd grown up in, and that was despite him playing in the Big Apple all these years. It worked for him, sitting there all laconic and relaxed, drawling his words and making Noah perk up.

I glanced at Stan, who was seated in another chair, his arms over his chest, his expression neutral.

"I love hockey," Noah murmured. "I want to play right wing like my dad."

Oliver chuckled. "God help the D-man who goes up against you then if you're like your dad." He shot me a wide smile, and I returned it, and Stan bristled. "So, I was fifteen, a bit older than you, when I got hit with the news. I thought it was the end of my hockey dreams. But here I am, a defenseman for the New York Thunder, and I've learned a thing or two about keeping my head in the game, both on and off the ice."

"What stops you from…" Noah made a motion with his hand like someone flopping to the floor, and then winced. "Sorry, I mean… I don't know how to describe it."

"You mean how do I stop a hypo, when my sugar levels drop too far, or hyper when they get too high? It's all about balance, and first off, I've got some tech on my side. I wear an insulin pump." He lifted his T-shirt, exposing a typical hockey player six-pack and his belly, to show a raised rectangle of white taped around the edge. "It's like a tiny, personal mechanic, always tweaking the amount of insulin I get." He dropped his shirt, and I swear Stan had been growling, then made it worse by tugging at a sleeve to show another thing fixed to his body. This time a slim pear-shaped device, again taped up, and with a plastic case on a band, which I assume protected it from knocks. "This is a continuous glucose monitor, a CGM, and believe me, you'll get to be an expert at learning what all these initials stand for."

"I have to learn those?" Noah looked lost.

I wanted to reach out and tell him that he didn't need to learn a damn thing if it made his life easier—yeah, I was losing my shit. Of course, he needed to learn this, and in fact everything.

"It will be second nature, I promise. Anyway, the CGM…" He paused and gestured at Noah.

"Uhmmm… Monitoring. Glucose. I forget the C."

"Continuous," Stan murmured, his voice gruff. "All time," he qualified.

Oliver shot Stan an amused glance. "Yeah, so the CGM is my buddy, always keeping an eye on my blood sugar levels, so I know exactly what's going on in my body. I can check it just by looking at my phone or even my smartwatch."

Noah's mouth fell open, "Like a video game HUD?"

"Yep, just like that. It's pretty cool stuff."

Noah's eyes widened. "I'd need a smartwatch," he said and stared at me, and then Stan.

"Will get you twenty," Stan offered, "All watch smarts. All kinds."

It made me happy to hear Stan engaged and not sulking, and this time when Stan glanced at me, he caught me looking and we exchanged soft, supportive, loving smiles.

"So, here's where it gets really space-age. I use

what's called 'hybrid looping.' It's where my CGM and pump talk to each other." He tapped his belly and his arm. "They're talking right now, and if my sugar's going high, the pump gives me more insulin. If I'm going low, it puts the brakes on. It's not perfect, but it's like having a co-pilot with me, twenty-four-seven."

"I'd be wearing those?"

"Maybe, I don't know what system you'll have, but it's one option, but what's important is that I can play hockey, and at NHL level."

"So, it's easy?" Noah sounded so hopeful.

Oliver shook his head. "I'm not gonna blow smoke up your…" Stan growled, and Oliver smirked. "Well… no. Diabetes is with you forever, and yeah it might mean you can't do some things, and some days you'll hate it, and other days you might want to tear all of this off and just feel normal. There's no easy fix, but work hard, look after yourself, and you'll be fine."

"But seriously, what about the NHL?" Noah asked after a pause. "I wanna play on the Railers like Papa and Dad."

"And I bet you will, and that's where it gets cool. On the team, we've got a nutritionist called Rainbow, and we work together to figure out what I should eat and when, especially on game days. Timing is everything with food, insulin, and exercise. She helps me stay at the top of my game without my levels going all rollercoaster on me. It's a team effort—and man, it works. Diabetes hasn't stopped me from staying in shape—if anything, it's made me pay more attention to my body, which is a good thing. I hit the gym, I skate, I do everything the other guys do. The only difference is that I've got to be a bit more on the ball with how my body's doing. I hide snacks everywhere, but, dude, don't hide them on the bench because that place is unhygienic."

Oliver glanced up at me, and I could read his expression, about how hard it might be, about the things he might not be saying, but the message here was that yes, Noah could play hockey. And that was all our hockey-mad pre-teen wanted to hear.

"And as for being a hockey player—that's about toughness, smarts, and heart. Diabetes doesn't touch that. It's not about whether you've got something extra to deal with; it's about how you handle it. I keep my head up, my stick down, and my eyes on the prize, just like you're gonna do."

"Okay."

"One shift at a time, just like on the ice. You learn to listen to your body, to work with it, not against it.

This is just a new part of your game plan, buddy. And you've got a whole team of people, including me, right behind you. I'll give you my number for if you have questions."

Noah's eyes grew super wide then. "For real?"

"Sure." He leaned close to Noah. "Members of the diabetes club stick together, and we have all kinds of cool things that your dads will never know about." He waggled his eyebrows theatrically, and I felt a million times lighter when Noah laughed.

He laughed.

"Noah, you're gonna make it work. You've just got to remember to look after yourself, keep track of your sugar, and never be shy about what you need to stay healthy. You do that, and there's nothing that can stop you—on the ice or off it."

"I have another question," Noah asked, and now he sounded unsure, and shy.

"Go for it."

"Can I still have things like pizza?" Noah's voice was hopeful, and I couldn't help but smile at the simplicity of his concern.

"Sure. It's all about moderation, but there's a ton of low-carb alternatives that I can talk to your dads about."

Noah sat up a little, and I could see the spark of confidence in him.

This was what I needed to see, what Stan needed, and I would owe Oliver for this.

He left a little after three, leaving a ton of Thunder merch with Noah, Margo, and a tongue-tied Eva who had arrived sometime after dawn, who immediately donned the jersey with Cowen's name on the back and did a whole lot of blushing.

Then with the girls off hunting for food in the cafeteria, it was just me, Noah, and Stan in the room.

"You okay?" I asked Noah, who nodded as he held the Cowen jersey wonderingly.

"I'm gonna play for the Railers," he said, and passed the gift to Stan, who pretended to throw it in the garbage, only stopping when I snatched it out of his hands.

Laughing Noah was brighter, happier, and when Stan laced his hand with mine, I felt as if maybe we could handle everything.

They wouldn't let us stay another night, or rather Noah demanded he wanted to be on his own, and the staff backed him up. Stan and I were reluctant to leave but when we were home and the girls were in bed, we hugged each other close.

And then it hit me what I needed to say.

"I want us to be there for Noah, for the girls. Always."

He eased me away and tried to read my expression. "We will be," he murmured.

"Nah, I'm done with hockey, Stan. I want something else now, and I know we should talk, but it's time for me to stop." I pressed a finger to his lips when he began to talk. "I'm retiring."

Chapter Nine

STAN

To say that I was shocked to my core would not describe how stunned Erik's announcement had left me. Easing out of the embrace, I sat back, my eyes wide, and moved myself around a bit on the sofa to stare at him.

"This is…" I scrambled to locate the proper words. "When is… what is this news?" Ugh, that was so not good English. I mumbled in Russian then tried again. "What is this striking out of the blue?"

Erik, knowing the talk he had mentioned was likely going to start now, breathed out a lungful of air that seemed to go forever.

"I know it seems like it's out of the blue, but it's not." He rose, waved at me to sit, and then padded off to the kitchen where I assumed he was going to make coffee. Two dogs took his place on the couch, furry heads coming to rest on my thigh. I sat there petting Bruno and Louisa. King was on the floor, his old hips keeping him from leaping up. I could sympathize.

I stared at the wall, lost in the suddenness of my husband's decision. Erik returned with two cups of coffee, passed me mine, and then shooed the dogs to the floor. They went to their beds, but they were not pleased.

"So, yeah, I'm sorry I sprang that on you," he confided, settling down then tucking a throw pillow under his left arm as he liked to do. It eased a lingering ache in his shoulder if he propped it, he claimed. "I know it must seem as if I just came to this radical decision but that's not the case."

"Then what is your case?" I asked, realizing my query sounded angry. I was not angry. I was stunned. Okay, maybe I was a little angry. Were married couples not to discuss major life decisions with each other before they were made? "I'm sorry to be sniping like irritated Chi-Chi dog but I am… how did you not talk with me about this before you just make snapping decision?"

"I *am* talking to you," he declared softly, taking a sip of coffee, his beautiful eyes showing all the exhaustion he felt.

"*Now*. You are talking now after making the big announcing," I snapped, my grip on my mug tightening. "I am not understanding how you make this call. Please, light me."

He smiled into his mug, his serenity in the face of my irritation making me more annoyed. I slurped my coffee, hoping he had made it improperly, but he had not.

"I'm sorry if you feel left out, that is not the case at all. Of course, I'm not going to just retire and not discuss it with you. That's what we're doing. I want to retire, Stan. I'm not like you, I'm a fourth line winger who works hard and loved hockey, until I didn't. It was a job, and I was damn good at it, but you're a star, Stan, the Olympics, you were an All-Star pick, you've got two Vezina's under your belt, you're different to me. I've lost the spark, and it happened in a single moment when I came home to paramedics at our house. I'm tired, and my body aches all the time."

"Mine aches also! Mine is newly chopped and made into *Terminator* hips. I suffer far more than you for many years, but I do not just quit."

"So, it's a competition of who hurts the worst?"

My gaze flew from my coffee to him. He studied me calmly. "What? No, of course it is not such a thing." I pulled in a steadying breath as the faint sounds of Mama's TV filtered through the now quiet house. "We all hurt. That is fact. Hockey makes hurt. But you have many years of good play left."

"I don't want to play anymore, Stan. I want to be with our kids. No one in this house saw the warning signs Noah was displaying." His gaze grew watery. He turned to stare at the pictures on the mantle, shots of our family over the years. The children as they grew and changed, dogs and cats that had filled our lives with love who were now in pet heaven, a wedding picture of my beloved and myself in Vegas after tying our knots. So many good memories. "My son was sick, and I didn't even notice."

"I also did not note. I too feel badly for my bad parenting."

Erik's hand brushed my whiskery cheek. I had not shaved for several weeks. My playoff beard was still hugging my face even though our dreams of achieving that goal were now over.

"Hey, no more guilt, right? We were all busy. Even your mother didn't pick up the signs and she's here with the kids all the time. But that being said, this situation with Noah, even though he will be fine and go on to achieve great things, has opened my eyes, Stan. It scared me. Deeply."

"It scared me too, but I am not rushing into such a big thing," I confessed, turning my nose into his palm to kiss his life line. "Why are we making life changes so big at all the once? I am scared of so much changes, Erik."

He moved closer, took my mug from my hand, and enveloped me in another embrace. "I know. Change is hard. It's been a long few days. Why don't we just snuggle and talk about this later?"

"Yes, okay." I brushed my lips over his, then tucked him into my side, both of us willing to stall a talk that, it seemed, one of us was not willing to have. I was too tired for deep analyzing of my boorish behavior right now. Tomorrow I would begin to pick apart my confused thoughts. Tonight, I wished to hold my husband close and plan other things for the return of our boy to our lives for Noah was coming home on the morrow. That was the important thing. Not my fears, upsets, or creeping worries about my own career. Family first. Always. Had I forgotten this most important thing and if I had what did that say for me and those I loved the most?

We celebrated the Fourth of July loudly and with many low-carb foods.

The past few weeks had been jumbly big time. All of us were working hard to ensure whatever Noah needed Noah got. Erik and I discussed hiring a cook/dietician to prepare diabetic-friendly meals and snacks. Mama cried when we told her. She said that her old cooking might have killed her little rabbit, which was of course not true, so we had to console her. Finally, after many tears we convinced her that all of us could eat better. Sure, Erik and I ate well because we were athletes. Or some of us were. One of us was. Maybe none of us were? I was confused and guilty still.

But for Mama's sake we compromised and brought in a dietician to work with Mama to relearn her old ways of preparing foods. While much of what Mama made—soups, cabbage, and salads—were good, much of the carbohydrates we ate which spiked Noah's levels had to go. He was allowed a little of things, but we were trying our hardest to help him learn new ways of eating. Still, my people did love our potatoes. Also, I had a great fondness for Mama's pierogi. The foods of Russia are as hearty as the people who live in that rugged land. They eat hearty foods that will stick to your ribs for when you journey out into temperatures that dip to minus forty Fahrenheit as it can in my homeland—you need lots of calories to sustain you.

Living here in America, in the lap of luxury, we did not need to eat like Siberian farmhands. And so, we were learning new ways to cook, which was benefitting us all. Still, I did yearn for pierogi and had stopped once or twice or several times after physical therapy at a small Slavic deli on Walnut Street near the police bureau building to buy some then eat them in the car. I was now back to driving myself to my appointments and walking with canes, which was wonderful, but the ice seemed a million miles away. The therapists could not give me a set time for when I could return to hockey.

"Give it time, Stan," Lance would say while sending notes to the Railers organization about me and my slow healing. It was frustrating so I ate pierogi to make me feel better, which of course they did. How could mashed potatoes in dough make you feel anything but warm and loved? Still, I knew I was sneaking bad foods so then I would feel guilty. It was foolish. I was foolish. Pierogi? No, they were not foolish. They were gifts from God.

Today I had not stopped to buy pierogi after therapy. I did blow kisses to the deli as I drove past it, but I stayed the course because we were making a trip with the children to West Virginia for the first part of a two-stage orientation for Eva. Margo was not coming as she was off at a week-long soccer camp in New Hampshire with several members of her school team and the coach. So, it was Eva and Noah, Erik and myself. Mama was pet-sitting and enjoying a long weekend alone.

When I pulled into the driveway Erik was just placing the last of our bags into the rear of his new Cadillac SUV. I exited my car, smiling, and made my slow way to my husband.

"I rushed as fast as Lance would allow," I explained then stood back as he closed the tailgate.

"No rush. It's not that far and we have all day." Erik stole a kiss, his eyes glowing with good health. Gone was the haunted look he had carried for so long after Noah's diagnosis. Now, with things starting to feel a bit more normal, he had blossomed. We had not talked about retirement again, and I had no idea if he even still felt the same way. He'd not said anything to the Railers, so perhaps he had changed his mind. I was not pushing. Things were starting to feel somewhat normal. "I thought maybe you might have stopped at Alexi's Deli for some pierogi." My mouth dropped. Erik snickered. "You tend to leave take out containers under the seat of your car."

"No, I do not leave, I hide." That made him laugh aloud and I joined in. "I am bad diet man."

"Nah, it's all good." He glanced around the vibrant green yard of our massive home then leaned in even closer to whisper to me. "To be honest, I swing by McDonald's for fish sandwiches whenever I go to the pet supply store."

"We are a couple of sneakers," I snickered then stole a kiss.

"Get a room," Noah called, charging out of the house, his eyes sparkling with joy at getting away for a few days.

His journey had not been an easy one. We still had days where his sugar spiked or dropped, and other days when he just felt blasé or sad, but overall, he was creeping towards being his old self. Next week, if his doctor okayed it, he would return to skating. Exercise was good for keeping sugar in check, I kept telling myself as I fretted over someone hitting him and knocking one of his new contraptions off or hurting him in some way. He was still too young for the roughest aspects of the game. Just. He would move into the next tier soon though, and that would involve full bodychecking. I knew I could not keep him in bubble wrap, but I dearly wished I could.

"Do you have all of your supplies?" I asked as Erik, and I broke apart.

"Yes, Papa," Noah sing-songed back as he climbed into the back seat, phone, and earbuds in hand, to wait for Eva to emerge from the house.

"Let me see," Erik insisted, and I winced. Noah wouldn't like that interfering from my beloved.

But no. Noah held out the black case, and he and Erik checked everything carefully, their heads bent, both with golden curls.

"Where is Eva? Is she coming with us?" I teased after ten minutes passed. Noah was complaining about the delay. Yes, he was feeling chipper today. I was always glad to see the bloom in his cheeks. Mama had done well for breakfast. Lots of healthy foods for all.

"I'll go check," Erik said, slid down out of the SUV and paused at the hood as Eva came jogging out of the house—at last—her long dark hair free, her smile wide. She was such a beauty. The boys at West Virginia Wesleyan College would be gaga. Perhaps I too should retire and go to live in the same dorms that Eva would be moving into, just to keep the slobbering jackals from her door. "We were about to call the Marines for a search mission."

"Ha, ha," Eva replied then climbed into the back seat where she then poked her little brother in the side. Noah giggled. I smiled at the two of them over the back of my seat. Such a sweet and kind big sister she was. I turned from the children to find Erik looking at me. We both managed weak smiles for each other. "I got a last-minute text from Lori. She's going to meet us on campus tomorrow morning."

"Ah good." I buckled up as Erik slid behind the wheel. "Lori is strong and sure friend. You and she will have lots of good study sessions."

"Lori and her will be too busy kissing guys to study," Noah said and got another poke in the ribs from his sister. I did note that she did not deny the fact that she and her best friend would, in fact, be kissing boys and not studying.

"Kissing boys is fun," Erik tossed out.

"See, Dad knows. Kissing boys is fun. Oh, Papa, don't scowl so. I'll study hard I promise," she said in that way she had of making me roll my eyes in a most fatherly way.

"Boys are off the limits until you graduate," I repeated my tried and true tested reply. "And then only after when you are making good moneys for high-ranking child psyching. And own home. And then find one boy who is good and kind to marry."

"So, I'm only allowed one guy after I'm thirty?" Eva teased and I nodded. "What about girls?"

Erik threw me a raised eyebrow as he cranked the engine over.

"Girls are okay as long as they do not make you not get big job making children's brains happy."

"I'll keep that in mind," she said with a naughty wink that made me shake my head.

"Did anyone bring any snacks?" Noah asked. "What? We ate like hours ago. If Eva hadn't been putting on lipstick and eyeshadow to impress the toll-taker on the turnpike maybe we could have left when we were supposed to."

"Look in the bags in the back. There's some baby carrots and a dish of ants on a log that Nana packed for you," I said, then gave Erik a look. "We are not out of the driveway yet and he is hungry."

"Just a normal, growing boy," Erik replied with a glowing smile.

Yes, that he was. A beautiful *healthy*, growing boy. And we would do everything within our powers to ensure he stayed that way.

Chapter Ten

ERIK

The morning sun filtered through the kitchen blinds, casting a warm glow over the quiet space where Stan was sipping his coffee. He hadn't heard me walk in, and I took a moment to watch him, the way his eyes crinkled when he concentrated on the crossword puzzle, always at a loss for the American words he needed to find. I'd once told him he should find Russian crosswords to do, but he was adamant working out random clues made his English better. He was wearing a Railers hoodie with his number and in Russian пять written under it. It meant five, for him, me, Noah, Margot, and Eva, and it was on all of his merchandise.

His family.

Looking at him, I felt a rush of emotions. Love, obviously, a deep all-consuming love as natural to me as breathing. There was admiration too, for the man he was, for the father he was, evident in every word he spoke. His resilience had been inspiring, his hockey awed me, and in all things he was mine and I was his. I didn't believe for one minute what I had to say to him now would change how we felt about each other, but still, I was scared. Part of me, a very small part of me, wondered if not having hockey to connect us may be a splinter that began to break us apart. I pushed that down. Stan and I were solid.

Still, I felt a pang in my chest knowing the news I was about to share might disrupt this peaceful scene. The kids were all out for one reason or another, Mama was at a neighbor's place for her weekly coffee and gossip, and we were alone.

"Stan," I began, my voice steady despite the turmoil inside.

He glanced up and smiled, then tapped his pen on the book. "One word. Five letters. Rhyme for herb."

I crossed to him, leaned over the book. "So, you have a Y?"

"Why?"

"The Y you have."

"Why is so hard," he moaned, and I chuckled.

"No, you have a letter. Y. In the middle."

He frowned, and stared, and then shrugged. "Y, Z, P, whatever, is too hard."

"Okay, rhyming herb, what rhymes with herb?"

He winced. "Umm… Brerb, Flerb, Glerb."

"Those are not words, sweetheart."

He muttered something in Russian. "Stupid," he added on the end.

I pressed a kiss to his hair. "What about an herb that rhymes with rhyme."

He stared at me, so close, he was almost cross-eyed. "Why not say that?" he demanded, and I kissed him on the end of his nose this time, and he was waylaid, buried his hands in my hair and tugged me in for a proper kiss. Then he released me just as fast. "Thyme!" He scribbled in the word and tossed his pencil to the counter. "Done."

"You've only filled in four clues."

His eyes darkened and he turned on the stool to widen his legs and tug me between them. "No stupid words crossing, more kissing."

I could have gone with that. I could have melted into his hold and lost myself in kisses and avoided the elephant in the room, but that wasn't the right thing for either of us. I pulled back a little. His eyes were closed as he chased for more kisses. I'd never seen anyone so beautiful in my life, and what I was doing might just break his heart.

"We need to talk."

"No talking, kissing."

I pressed a hand to his chest, and waited, as he stared up at me, his brow furrowed, sensing the seriousness of the conversation. "What?"

I took a deep breath, the weight of my decision pressing down on me. "I'm going to call a meeting with team management today. It's time for me to retire from playing hockey with the Railers."

"We haven't talked," he said.

"Every time I try to talk to you, I just can't get the words out," I whispered. "I just need to do this, and I want you to still love me even if I—"

He pressed a finger to my lips. "I love you forever."

"Then you'll do this with me? Come with me?" This was a moment I'd rehearsed a thousand times in my head, but now that it was here, it felt surreal.

He closed his eyes for a moment, but his jaw tensed, and I knew he was fighting that demon that told him we'd be playing hockey forever, that it was in our DNA, that we'd be sixty and still playing.

"My beloved…" His gray eyes were stormy with emotions, but I couldn't let him waylay this any longer. The Railers deserved to know, the kids too, and I was doing this one way or another.

"I know you hate it," I continued, reaching for the press release I had prepared—the tangible proof of what I wanted to do. "But I've poured everything into this decision. It's not just made because I'm tired. I'm not disillusioned, I love the game, I love the Railers, but I want to go, before there's even a hint of being traded."

He snarled. "You go, I go."

"That isn't the point Stan. Look, read this." I handed the press release to him, and as he read it to himself, I watched the emotions play across his face —surprise, understanding, and then a soft pride that made my heart swell. Then he read it again, this time out loud, in halting words, and with so much emotion I wanted to cry.

"To my Railers family and the incredible fans,

Today, with a heart full of mixed emotions, I am announcing my retirement from professional hockey. This game has been my lifeblood, my passion, and my teacher. It has shaped me into the man I am today, and for that, I am eternally grateful.

I have been blessed to spend my days playing with an extraordinary group of men, my band of brothers, who not only stood beside me on the ice but also helped me raise my son and supported me in finding the greatest love with my husband, Stan.

Every single day with the Railers was a day lived to the fullest, a dream I had the privilege to experience. As I hang up my skates, I look forward to the future with excitement. My plans are many, but they all start with family. With Stan. With the one man who has shown me what shape my forever will be.

To the younger players, the ice is yours now. Step up, play hard, and carry on the Railers legacy we've all worked so hard to build.

To the fans, your cheers, your faith, and your unwavering support have been the soundtrack of my career. I might be stepping away from the game, but I will never lose my love for this sport, nor will I forget the memories and the joy you have brought into my life.

Thank you, from the bottom of my heart.

Let's Go Railers.

Erik Gunnarson-Lyamin"

Stan kissed me then, cradled my face, his eyes bright with emotion, then he nodded. "Let's go."

The moment I waved Stan off to the first pre-season game of the new season was the worst for many reasons. I already missed him as soon as the gates closed behind his SUV, and the surreal feeling I should be going with him would probably linger for a while. It was also the worst day because even this late in September he wasn't cleared to play, still on long-term injured reserve, and today he would be meeting Lincoln Hearth, the new kid traded in from Seattle, to be second goalie, backing up Bryan. The team had reassured Stan that as soon as he was back he'd have a role, but it couldn't be just me who read between the lines with the fact they hadn't said he'd be starting goalie.

And when *exactly* was he going to be fit enough to play?

He was walking, running, pushing weights, but still using meds when the pain was too bad, still having PT, still seeing the surgeon for post-surgery care and advice.

Yet, he was determined to play.

And knowing Stan, he would, because there was nothing he couldn't do if he put his mind to it. It wasn't on me to suggest he retire as well, that would be all on my incredibly stubborn, highly talented and marketable husband. I sighed, aware that I still hadn't seen Noah.

Noah's low sugar alarm had sounded twice in the night, but it was because he'd rolled onto the sensor on his arm and compressed it. He had a case that strapped over it, but sometimes not even that stopped the compression. I knew he'd wake up tired, but that was just part of getting used to his new normal. He was a bright, sunny kid, and he went with the flow.

"Kids! Breakfast! We need to go soon!" I called up to them, but Margo was in the girls' bathroom with the blow-dryer on and music blaring from her phone, so I probably wasn't being heard. I headed upstairs, feeling a bit lost not to be rounding up three kids as Eva was now on campus and giddy with delight at being on her own. Stan and I had an Eva-sized hole in our hearts, but we were so damned proud of our daughter. Rapping at the door, I waited until the music quieted, and the blow-dryer stalled as Margo cracked the door.

"Thirty minutes until we have to leave," I reminded her.

"Okay, Dad." The door closed, the music went back up and the hair dryer was back on.

Then I crossed to Noah's bedroom. We'd always

had this policy of never just walking in, but since the diagnosis both Stan and I had become extra vigilant, and if he didn't immediately answer then we knocked again, waited, then went in. This morning was no different. After all, he had to get to school as well, and the clock was running down. I'd heard his shower, so assumed he'd at least made it out of bed, but he needed to get some breakfast and therefore I had to be the bad guy. His door was slightly open anyway, but I still knocked.

"Noah?"

I heard a noise that sounded like come in, and assumed it was okay to go inside, but I made sure to do it noisily… just in case.

"Huh?" Noah asked, his back to the window, staring at me, a little unfocused. He was dressed for school, his Chesterford Academy uniform neat, his tie knotted, although crooked.

"Hey, buddy, let's get downstairs for breakfast. I'm making pancakes."

"I uhm…" He blinked at me. "I can't find… my tie…"

"You're wearing it," I began, ready to tease him, but then the muffled sound of an alarm broke the thought, and I realized it was the alarm for low sugar. Where was his phone? Why wasn't he wearing his watch? The alarm sounded as if it came from his bed, and I dug through the covers, pulling out what I needed, and then crossed to Noah, who was still staring around him searching for his tie. I pressed a Skittle into his hand from the small supply I always had now, stored in a tiny case, and told him to eat it. Each Skittle was one gram of carbs, and I tried to recall what would pull his levels up, checking the graph, working out all the complicated things we needed to watch for, then handed him three more. He ate them as I pressed a hand to his damp forehead. "You're hypo," I said, not sure he understood, then I sat him down on the bed, and kept him company, until *finally* the sugar made its way into his bloodstream and back up to his brain, and he blinked as he turned to me.

"Okay," he murmured, glancing down at his tie. "I'm okay."

"Pancakes," I advised, ruffling his curls, making him huff and shove me away, and he followed me downstairs, Margo already down in the kitchen waiting. "Margo, I'll call the school, because we're going to be late today."

"That's not fair," Margo whined, "I don't wanna miss English."

"We all need breakfast, and your brother wasn't feeling so good."

She sniffed and then returned to eating her pancakes, and I waited for her to complain that they weren't normal ones and how it was unfair she had to eat what Noah did. Instead, she reached out and squeezed Noah's hand in silent support then hugged him from the side.

I could have cried. My throat was so tight, and I had to cough to clear it. They didn't want to watch their dad lose his shit over Stan leaving, and Noah having a hypo and me not knowing what I was going to do with myself.

"Don't forget you both have sports practice after school," I told Margo and Noah, both of them wanting to play for the Chesterford Coyotes teams—soccer and hockey respectively—both of them probably going to make it, and yes, I was biased, but they were both good. "I thought about dropping in, maybe to volunteer to help coach hockey this season, just the assistant, and I won't interrupt you with what you're… but look… is that okay with you?"

Both Noah and Margo stared at me, their eyes wide. My chest tightened. The last thing they would want was their dad there messing things up.

Then Noah nodded. "Cool."

And Margo grinned. "Way cool."

Volunteering to be an assistant coach for the Chesterford Coyotes seemed as if it was a step in the right direction in finding out what I wanted the shape of the rest of my life to be outside of family.

I wish Stan could be there with me.

Chapter Eleven

STAN

"But, Papa, Dad is already committed to the hockey team, and our soccer club is really desperate for someone."

I looked up over my e-reader, my glasses on my nose, to find my middle child giving me her best sad Puss-in-Boots face.

"They are so desperate for a coach that you come to me?" I teased.

Margo's face fell. "No, no, Papa, no! You were the first choice!" She wiggled onto the sofa beside me, her ponytails dangling down on either side of her slim face, the very image of a pleading cherub. "I told Coach Nancy that you played soccer as a young boy and before every game when you were a Railer."

"I am still a Railer, Margo," I explained patiently.

Perhaps if I said it often enough, even I would start to believe it. Being on LTIR was frustrating. My therapy was not moving at the rate anyone wished it to be, and while I was now mobile, I was still not on skates. Halloween was in two weeks and here I sat, reading a spooky gay romance novel as my team—with the new addition of the young goalie with the good hips—Lincoln Hearth from Illinois—were off to a great start of a new season.

"Well, yes," she replied sheepishly, tucking her legs under her backside to sit on her heels. I used to be able to sit like that. Now I doubted I would ever be as bendy as I used to be. "But you are sitting out for months yet. If you could fill in for the fall and winter seasons I know by spring they'll have someone else, and you can go play hockey if you're still able."

I wanted to tell her that I would be able, of course I would, but deep down in my heart I had massive doubts. Also, and this was a niggling thing that was growing bigger every day, I was starting to enjoy being home with my husband and children. Mama now had more time to enjoy her golden years with Erik off the roster. We had a trip planned for over the holidays, a journey to California with the children to visit Disneyland then play in the ocean for a few days.

The Railers were facing off with the Storm, just

one of two times the teams met. Usually, I would be in net but now, for the first time in years, I could enjoy family time. It was appealing, and each day found me less and less keen to return to the game. I'd not spoken of this to anyone yet. It was unlike me to be so indecisive. Perhaps I would discuss it with Galina when she and Arvy arrived for the first home game of the year where the Railers had a goodbye event planned before the game with the Rebels. A montage for Erik, filled with memories of his days playing hockey, images of him and me, the children, his work with local charities. It would be a nice thing and he was thrilled to be honored in such a way. The fans were saddened at his announcement but had rushed to buy tickets to the game.

Would the fans be sad if I said I were leaving? Would the team create a nice montage for me when I left? If. *If* I left.

"Papa, are you checking your eyelids for holes again?"

I snapped back to my child. "No, I was walking in the sheep pasture in my head cutting the wool."

"So, about soccer coaching?" she wheedled, her lower lip hanging out so far, a parrot could have landed on it.

"Fine, I will step in for a short time but—"

She squealed then launched herself at me, hugging me so tight around the neck I asked if she were trying to put me into the famous Roddy Piper sleeper hold. She giggled, kissed my cheek, and then ran off to text her friends. I expected a call from Coach Nancy any second. Smiling to myself, I sat back, adjusted my glasses, and then heard Erik coming in with the pack from a light run around the local dog park.

Tags on collars jangled as the dogs filed into the living room, bright-eyed and bushy-tailed, with Erik bringing up the rear looking exhausted.

"Good thing I talked you out of taking them. King spotted a squirrel and that led to a dog stampede where several pooches leapt the fence," he said as he dropped down beside me, his curls a mess but his cheeks pink. "It was bedlam. Mrs. Minerva, the fortune teller who lives down the street with her son Mike the investment manager, was totally unprepared for her Yorkie— Tittles—to break free of the enclosure. Which makes me wonder how good of a clairvoyant she is if she didn't know about the doggie prison break in advance."

"She told me that my life would change in a bigly way at Mike's last neighborhood barbecue."

"Well to be fair, Stan, that's kind of vague. She

also told me that I'd discover a long-lost relative who wanted to help me write a screenplay about a porcupine that tap danced."

"That is not vague at all," I pointed out as he toed off his sneakers then turned to face me. I'd built a nice fire to counter the cold air of fall. My knees ached badly as soon as the temperature dipped below fifty. Those joints were also shot from hockey, but I was not ready to have them replaced yet. I'd been so long just getting to the point where I was almost back to normal that the mere thought of going under the knife again gave me bad dreams.

"No, but it's not happened yet either."

"Perhaps it will. Premonitions do not come with expiration dates," I reminded him while the dogs padded around then settled in front of the fireplace on the big hearth rug. "Margo asked me to coach her soccer team."

"Oh?"

That was all he said. I waited but he didn't speak again.

"Is that all your words?"

"I just…" He rolled his lips over his teeth before speaking. "Okay, so this is just my two cents, and you can take it or leave it."

"I will never leave your pennies," I assured him.

His mouth pulled up into a tender smile. "That's good to know. Okay, so hear me out. I'm not pressuring you into anything, and I know how badly you want to get back on the ice."

"Meh," I mumbled, and his eyes flared.

"What?"

"Listen to this." I straightened my left leg. The knee popped. I winced. The same thing happened when I stretched out my right leg, only that one ground inside just like my hips used to do before cracking like tinder. "Bad joints. More bad joints. More surgery. More recovery."

"You don't have to get your knees done now, babe," he said, taking my left hand between his.

"I think maybe I'm done," I said after a pause.

"Done with hockey?"

"I am not saying that. I am just…" I blew out a short breath. "I am having a hard time with my brain deciding how to go, or which path to take. Being here with you and the children is amazing. I love our daily things, little things like dog-walking or grocery shopping or just strolling downtown to get coffee hand in hand."

"I love those too," he confirmed as he wiggled his fingers between mine.

"But I also am missing the team, the ice, my

pipes. Did you know that Lincoln does not speak to them? What must they be thinking?!"

"I'm sure the pipes understand that you're injured."

"Hmm, I am not so sure of that. I am not so sure of anything and that is scary."

"You'll figure it out, and no matter what you choose, returning to hockey next season or calling it quits, we'll all be there with you." He kissed my scarred knuckles then took his spot under my arm. I buried my nose into his curls. Maybe I should go talk to Mrs. Minerva and see what she saw for my future.

Perhaps I would after a few days so that she could forget that my dog had led a canine escape from Alcatraz. I did not want a soothsayer mad at me. They could hex a man so that his peter would wither up and fall off. Mama knew such things to be true and had passed along her knowledge to her two children. I spat twice over my shoulder—the one minus Erik's head—just in case.

"I think I know where my heart lies," I whispered into his curls.

"Want to tell me?" he asked and so I did.

The day of Erik's celebration I went to morning skate.

Not to skate as my hips were not quite up to that, but to spend some time with the team as I had in the old days. Also, I had to speak to my oldest and dearest friends.

"Privet," I called as I made my way across the ice. No one was at the practice arena yet. I'd gotten up early with Erik when Noah's sugar alarm went off at five a.m. Somedays it felt as if we had this diabetes under control, and then some days it felt as if it had us on the run. We'd gotten the children back to sleep, finally, and Erik and Mama as well, but I'd not been able to find rest, so I had dressed, let the dogs out, fed the cats, and then drove across town to the practice facility to have a long, hard talk. "I think you might be mad at me?" I asked the pipes in Russian.

They acted sullen.

These were the ones at the Railers end of the ice, silent under a low spotlight, the rest of the rink dimly lit as I had asked Milton—the Railers maintenance expert—to do for me. Milton and I went way back because he had been here for many years. We'd shared cocoa and doughnuts back in the day.

I moved to the pipes, touching them with bare fingers. They were icy cold. Solid, dependable, and a part of me. Sometimes, when I was in that twilight place between sleep and wakefulness, I could feel them resting on my back. Always there, always sturdy, always on guard.

"I know it has been some time, and that new people have been here," I whispered, trailing my fingertips along their dented frames. The red paint nicked here and there. "Some of the people who are here do not speak to you. I have told Bryan and Lincoln they must talk to you in Russian. I think they may be talking in English but that is okay, no?"

I ran my hand over the netting, inhaling the smell of the ice. Brittle, cold air touched my cheeks. I let my eyes close as I wrapped my fingers around the crossbar then breathed in and out as if I were Mrs. Minerva reaching out to those on the other side. She'd told me that my life was about to change.

"Do not hold their lack of Russian against them for Bryan and Lincoln are good goalies. They will need your help. I know, I know." I gave the cold pipe a squeeze. "It is not always easy to say goodbye, but I think… well, my friend, I think it might be time for me to let the new tenders guard your opening." I paused. "That sounded bad. But I am tired, my friend, and my children need me. Noah is still trying to come to terms with his disease, Margo is about to be fourteen and is in the process of transitioning, so she needs her Papa there for her now more than ever. Eva is grown now and gone but she calls every day and I want to be able to go visit her when the mood strikes. I miss Galina and my little nieces. Mama is not as spry as she once was and Erik... well, he is happy now. I see that joy in him every day and I think that I wish to have that peace in my heart." I rubbed the cold bar. "Do not feel badly for missing me. We had our time. Now it is for the best that you allow other men into your... I am not sure that will sound much better. I will come visit I promise. I will play in alumni games often so that we can catch up. I will never abandon you. It is just that my family needs me now. I am weary. My soul needs rest, my body is worn out. Please, do be good to the men who follow me. They are Railers."

I bent down to kiss the crossbar.

"Do you two need a minute?" I heard Tennant calling from somewhere behind me. I turned to find him smirking at me from the home bench still in his street clothes. Our captain. My dearest friend. It seemed right that I speak with Tennant before I go to the coach then to the owner.

I shook my head. "No, I think we are done. I would like to speak with you though if you are having a minute?"

My best friend nodded; his expression wary. I smiled for him then turned to the pipes.

"You may need to learn English," I told them.

I gave them a final pat then made my way with care to Tennant so we could talk.

And it was Ten who hugged me after and walked to the car with me.

"Gonna miss you, Stan," he said, his eyes damp.

I tugged him close. "I will visit all days," I said, choked. "For pipes."

Tennant grinned. "For the pipes. Sure."

Epilogue

Erik

NHL draft – Noah's year

The excitement in the Railers arena was a humming energy vibrating through the soles of my feet and into my chest. It seemed like fate that this year's NHL draft was being held in the very arena where we'd played and trained for so many years. Up in the rafters, Stan's number had been retired, one of the greatest goalies in the team, and the game. I was proud of him, and the Railers, and Noah, and I couldn't help leaning forward, elbows on my knees, eyes fixed on the stage where Noah's future would be unveiled. I could feel Stan's knee pressed against mine, a solid presence grounding me amidst the nerve-wracking anticipation. We'd had the first round, and none of us were surprised when Noah wasn't taken that time—he was a solid second round choice, and that wasn't a bad thing, the weight of expectation given his two former NHL dads was high enough without adding more pressure.

Noah sat along from me, next to Stan, trying to look calm, but I could see the tell-tale bounce of his knee, the way he fiddled with the sleeve of his jacket, and the constant checking of his watch for his sugar levels. He was a right wing, just like me, and I was so proud I could burst. I swear I could barely keep my pride in check, a swelling tide that threatened to spill over in a whoop or a holler when his name was called —inappropriate, sure, but the kids were everything to us, and Noah's journey hadn't been easy.

He'd chosen the college route, Michigan, and it suited him. It made him grow, not just in his game but as a man. And now, in his second year, there we were at the draft, the second round ticking closer. Noah's dream, our shared dream, was a whisper away from becoming reality.

"Jiggering, juddering, rabbit," Stan muttered, and clasped my hand, his other right over the T-shirt he wore under his jacket with the picture of a rabbit. Noah had gotten it for him as a joke, but Stan was so damn emotional and proud about it he'd worn it today in lieu of a shirt. Not many people knew what he'd used to call Noah—what he still called Noah—but it was us, and it was real.

"Me too."

"Is all over. Like stamps and worms."

"Yeah." I squeezed his hand, and then leaned into him, my big man, as nervous as the day we'd walked Eva down the aisle with her man, Dan. Of course, for Stan it was half nerves, and half a reaction to threatening Dan that if he ever hurt Eva Stan knew people.

"It's okay," I reassured him, and caught Noah's smile as he saw us holding hands and being nervous together. I dropped my voice. "If Noah doesn't get the Railers, then Boston is up next, and after that the Raptors, all three wanted him."

"Is all Railers," Stan whispered back. "Please."

Tom was next to Noah, leaning in to mutter

something that had Noah cracking a brief smile. Tom, his nutritionist, and best friend always had that ability —to cut through tension with a well-timed joke or an irreverent comment. He'd been two years above Noah at college, but they'd met through hockey, and with his degree in nutrition Tom had taken on the role of Noah's informal PA as soon as he'd graduated, keeping an eye on his diabetes, and through that connection they'd become inseparable.

As the MC took position for the next team choice, the murmurs of the crowd settled into a hush of anticipation. It was the Railers' turn to take their next pick, and moment was heavy with the dreams of every young athlete in the room, but also for me and Stan. Then, with a clear and resonant voice that filled the arena, the announcer spoke:

"With their second pick in this year's NHL draft, the Railers are proud to select… from the University of Michigan, playing right wing, Noah Gunnarsson-Lyamin!"

I couldn't move, Stan's hand found mine, a grip that said everything—pride, relief, elation. Our son, our boy, was going to don the Railers jersey. There was thunderous applause, so much had been made about our son following us to the Railers, and all eyes were on Noah as he rose, a mix of disbelief and pride etched across his face. The moment was electric for Stan and me.

Noah hugged us both.

"Yes! Yes! Yes!" he shouted in our ears—his excitement palpable. "I'll prove they need to play me!" he added, and Stan and I held him tight and agreed with every word.

He hugged Tom, Eva and Dan, Margot, dipped to hug the man with the cap who glanced up at me with a twinkle in his eyes. Tennant Rowe was there for our son, still captain of the team he loved, and he hugged Noah, and Noah hugged him back as family cameras caught the moment for us.

Noah waited at the end of the aisle, and for a second our eyes met. All the mornings on the ice, the late-night practices, the sacrifices—it had all led to this. Then he walked to the stage, and I stood, Stan beside me, as he pulled the dusky blue of the Railers jersey, with his number on the back—my number— and took his first steps into his future.

The Railers. Home. It's more than just a team; it's a legacy.

And now Noah was going to be part of it.

Stan hugged me, I hugged him back, and we

shouted to Noah that we loved him, and probably embarrassed him completely, but it was everything.

It was love.

THE END

Read Noah's story, coming Fall 2024

When he's lost everything, can Michael rebuild his broken life and find a love worth fighting for?

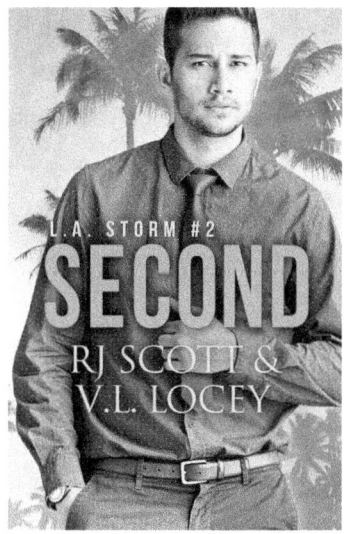

Second (LA Storm 2)

Read book 1, Script

In the high-stakes world of professional hockey, Michael "Zeetoo" Zhang once had the potential to shine even brighter than his older brother, captain of the LA Storm. But one wrong turn and a growing gambling habit have led him down a treacherous path. After a run of bad luck, he's left with nothing but debts, and after an arrest, he's slammed with a non-custodial sentence of work in the community. Fate takes an unexpected turn when he is placed in an inner-city garden project, where he encounters Bryce, the enigmatic and surly manager of the project, who harbors a deep resentment toward him. Despite Bryce's cold demeanor, Michael wants to prove himself worthy of being loved, if only the scars of past failures and the constant shadow of his brother's success didn't haunt him and leave him feeling lost and alone.

Bryce Kincaid is chased by his own brand of demons, and years out from his mistakes, he's determined to stick to one path and never waver, just in case he once again loses control. Michael Zhang is everything Bryce doesn't want in his life; temptation wrapped in sex, the hockey player is a man on the edge, and to fall for him would mean Bryce opening his heart to hurt.

As they work side by side, the walls around Bryce's heart begin to crack, revealing a vulnerability that even Michael can't resist. Drawn to each other they discover a passion that goes beyond the ice and the earth, and find a love that defies the odds. Only, just as Michael starts to believe in second chances, his past catches up with him, threatening to derail his life completely, and destroy Bryce right along with him. If he wants a life with Bryce then Michael must confront the demons of his past and fight for the future he never thought he deserved.

Read book 1, Script

Hockey Series' from RJ Scott & V.L. Locey

Harrisburg Railers

Owatonna U Hockey

Arizona Raptors

Boston Rebels

LA Storm

Chesterford Coyotes - Young Adult

Free Reads

Please note - in all of these free stories, there will be some spoilers for the main series books.

Railers Short Stories

Volume 1 | Volume 2

LA Storm

Sparkle

The Colts - AHL Short Stories

Pucks & Percentages

Breakaway

Making the Save

Standalone

Waiting for Christmas

When hockey wunderkind Tennant Rowe meets his new coach, he knows he's in trouble. Jared Madsen is nine years older than Tennant, impossibly attractive, and — worst of all — his brother's off-limits best friend. Is their chemistry worth the risk?

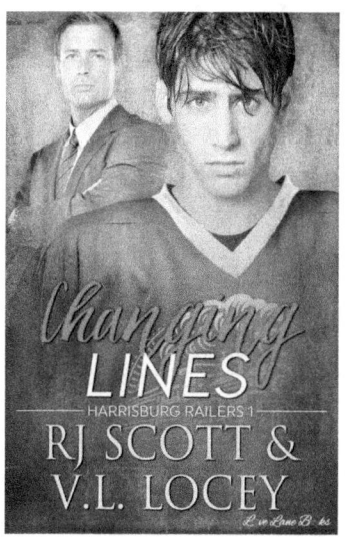

Changing Lines (Railers 1)

Can Tennant show Jared that age is just a number, and that love is all that matters?

The Rowe Brothers are famous hockey hotshots, but as the youngest of the trio, Tennant has always had to play against his brothers' reputations. To get out of their shadows, and against their advice, he accepts a trade to the Harrisburg Railers, where he runs into Jared Madsen. Mads is an old family friend and his brother's one-time teammate. Mads is Tennant's new coach. And Mads is the sexiest thing he's ever laid eyes on.

Jared Madsen's hockey career was cut short by a fault in his heart, but coaching keeps him close to the game. When Ten is traded to the team, his carefully organized world is thrown into chaos. Nine years his junior and his best friend's brother, he knows Ten is strictly off-limits, but as soon as he sees Ten's moves, on and off the ice, he knows that his heart could get him into trouble again.

Harrisburg Railers (Hockey Romance)

Railers Volume 1 | Railers Volume 2 | Railers Volume 3 | Railers Volume 4

Meet the men of Owatonna University's hockey team

Ryker (Owatonna U, 1)

Ryker is hockey royalty, Jacob is a poor country boy. Can two vastly different people find common ground and become the men they want to be?

Ryker comes from a long line of championship-winning hockey players. Playing college hockey to develop his game is his only focus, and nothing will stand in the way of him working to become the best player. He has no room for relationships, people who point out his flaws, or anyone who calls him on his dreams. He certainly has no place for love, and meeting Jacob is nothing but a useful distraction on the side. After all trying to get his Owatonna Eagles teammate into bed is less work and more play. When tragedy rocks his family, his charmed life crumbles, and the only person he can turn to is the same one who claims to hate him.

Jacob Benson has only known hard work and stifling conservative values his whole life. Born and raised in the small rural community of Eden Crossing, Minnesota, he's the only son of a hard-working but struggling dairy farming family. Jacob is using his skills in hockey to finance his way to an agricultural science degree. These four years at Owatonna U. will probably be the only time he has to enjoy life, gain acceptance about his sexuality, and live openly before his inevitable return to the farm. Running into a pretty rich boy like Ryker Madsen is putting a damper on his enjoyment of life away from home. Ryker's flip, conceited, carefree attitude grates on Jacob's every nerve. So why, if Ryker is everything he dislikes, does he want nothing more than to explore the sinful dreams that his annoying teammate stars in every night?

Ryker

Owatonna U Hockey (Hockey Romance)

Coast to Coast (Arizona Raptors 1)

Coast To Coast

When opposites attract, this bottom-of-the-league team will never be the same again.

A stipulation in his father's will forces Mark back into the arms of a family that disowned him and leaves him one-third owner of a hockey team facing financial ruin. He doesn't even watch hockey, let alone like it, and wants nothing more than to head back to New York. Then there's the new coach, a stubborn, opinionated, irritating man with superiority issues and questionable music taste. Butting heads with Rowen becomes the new normal, but it comes with passionate debate and an all-consuming lust.

Challenged to rebuild one of the worst teams in the league into a future cup contender, Rowen can't pass up the opportunity. Never in his twenty years of hockey has he ever seen a team managed so badly or coached players overflowing with resentment and bigotry. Yet there's something about this team and this city that compels him to roll up his sleeves and start dismantling. If only Mark, one of three siblings who now own the Raptors, wasn't so damned rock-headed yet so damned appealing his job might be easier. It doesn't look like either is willing to give in, but one night in a dark, desert hotel changes everything.

Coast To Coast

Arizona Raptors (Hockey Romance)

1. Coast To Coast
2. Across the Pond
3. Shadow and Light
4. Sugar and Ice
5. School and Rock

Boston Rebels

Top Shelf (Boston Rebels 1)

Acting on the attraction to his best friend's brother has always been off the table for Xander until a passionate hookup with Mason at a beach resort begins a love affair that burns long after summer ends.

Mason specializes in assisting same-sex couples on their journey to becoming parents and fighting every rule that blocks his way in the stuck-in-the-past agency that hired him. Living in his brother's pool house is rent-free, and every cent he earns he saves for his dream—that one day he'd have his own company helping others. The downside is that he has to see his annoying brother every day, the upside is that his brother's teammates from the Boston Rebels make regular visits. The eye candy that passes Mason's window is almost enough to make him consider dating a hockey player, but not just any player though. Ever since Xander—his brother's childhood friend—came out as gay at a press conference, Mason's puppy love has turned into a burning attraction he can no longer ignore.

Hockey has been one of Xander's main focuses since he was old enough to balance on skates. Well, hockey and Mason Kingsley, but Mason was always unattainable. Now that he's about to see thirty candles on his birthday cake and is no longer hiding the fact he's gay, he's ready to find a soul mate to make his life complete. A summer vacation is just what he needs to have time to think, but when the Boston Rebels arriving in paradise with Mason in tow, thinking is the last thing he needs. One torrid night under a balmy moon and rules about not messing with his best friend's brother vanish on a warm, tropical breeze.

Summer romances don't generally last past Labor Day, but with the new season about to begin Xander and Mason are going to have to face the world and decide if their love is real enough to withstand everything.

Boston Rebels

Lost In Boston (Free Prequel Novella)

1. Top Shelf
2. Back Check
3. Snowed
4. Royal Lines
5. Blade
6. Rental

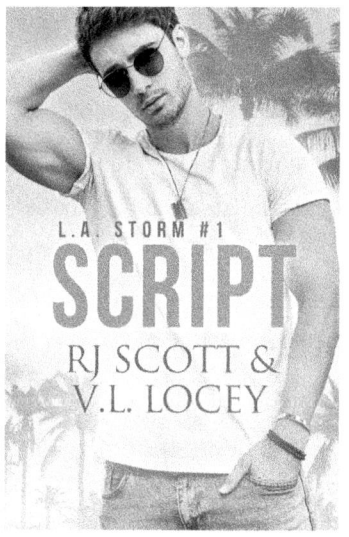

Script (LA Storm, 1)

Script

Hollywood A-lister Finn might be Canadian, but he needs Cameron to show him how to hockey.

Actor Finn Kerrigan is at a crossroads. After growing up a soap star, then starring in a hugely successful trilogy of action movies, he's finally given the chance to read a heartfelt and passionate script that could change his life forever. The role would be enough for people to see him as a serious actor, and maybe even win him an award or two (and no, a golden raspberry award for his action movies doesn't count). Once established as a serious actor he's sure he can come out of the closet and finally live his truth.

When he lies to get the part of a hockey player on a struggling team, he suddenly has nowhere to hide. He might be Canadian, but the last time he skated he was ten, and no, he doesn't have hockey in his blood. With only a month until filming starts, he about to be exposed, but partnered with a player who's supposed to be giving him tips, he doesn't realize how many of his secrets will come to light. Falling in lust, one heated kiss at a time, is inevitable, but giving Cameron up at the end of the shoot could break his heart.

Cameron Chavkin is the face of the LA Storm. And the body, and the hair, and the smile. He's at the prime of his career, men and women want to be with him, and he's skating better than he ever has before. His house sits next to a famous rock star's mansion, his garage is filled with expensive cars, and he's even been asked to mentor a once-famous actor in a new hockey movie. Life is pretty sweet. Until the bad boy of hockey meets Finn, a man on the edge with more secrets than Cameron has endorsements. Knowing better than to get involved, Cameron is swept up despite himself, and when it's time to say goodbye to the Storm's most eligible bachelor is finding it hard to follow the script.

Script

LA Storm

1. Script
2. Second
3. Shield
4. Spiral

Off The Ice (Chesterford Coyotes, 1)

Off The Ice

**A coming-of-age love story with high school, hockey
rivalry, friendship, family, and coming out.**

Soren's life changes in an instant when he and his younger
brother are adopted by hockey royalty. Making sense of his
new life is hard enough, but when he's enrolled in a private
school it means facing a whole new set of problems.

Navigating friendship, family, and hockey is one thing, but being attracted to the boy who vexes him is a whole new thing.

Felix has a reputation to protect. He's the kid who seems to have everything but looks can be deceiving. Spinning lies about his perfect life, he's created a fantasy world that even he has started to believe. Only, it's not long before everything crumbles, all of his pretty lies are revealed, and only his closest rival sees through his pain and stands by him.

Fighting is easy, friendship is hard, but love is everything.

Off The Ice

Chesterford Coyotes

1. Off The Ice
2. On Thin Ice
3. *Dance on Ice*

Also By RJ Scott

For a full list of ebooks and links please scan the code
above or visit rjscott.co.uk/rjbooks

Meet RJ Scott

RJ discovered romance in books at a very young age and realized that if there wasn't romance on the page, she could create it in her head. With over one hundred and fifty books published, she is a full time author of gay romance.

She lives and works out of her home in the beautiful English countryside, spends her spare time reading, watching films, and enjoying time with her family.

The last time she had a week's break from writing she didn't like it one little bit and has yet to meet a box of chocolates she couldn't defeat.

www.rjscott.co.uk | rj@rjscott.co.uk

NEWSLETTER - rjscott.co.uk/rjnews

facebook.com/author.rjscott

x.com/Rjscott_author

instagram.com/rjscott_author

amazon.com/author/rj-scott

bookbub.com/authors/rj-scott

goodreads.com/rjscott

pinterest.com/rjscottauthor

Also By VL Locey

For a full list of ebooks and links please scan the code
above or visit vllocey.com/stories-from-vl-locey

Meet V.L. Locey

V.L. Locey loves worn jeans, yoga, belly laughs, walking, reading and writing lusty tales, Greek mythology, the New York Rangers, comic books, and coffee.

(Not necessarily in that order.)

She shares her life with her husband, her daughter, one dog, two cats, a flock of assorted domestic fowl, and two Jersey steers.

When not writing spicy romances, she enjoys spending her day with her menagerie in the rolling hills of Pennsylvania with a cup of fresh java in hand.

vllocey.com
vicki@vllocey.com

Newsletter - vllocey.com/newsletter

facebook.com/V.L.Locey

x.com/vllocey

instagram.com/vl_locey

bookbub.com/authors/v-l-locey

goodreads.com/vllocey

pinterest.com/vllocey